THE WITHERED ARM
and other Wessex Tales

THE
WITHERED ARM
and other
Wessex Tales

THOMAS HARDY

With an introduction by Robert Gittings

Heinemann Educational Books Ltd
Halley Court, Jordan Hill, Oxford OX2 8EJ
OXFORD   LONDON   EDINBURGH
MADRID   ATHENS   BOLOGNA   PARIS
MELBOURNE   SYDNEY   AUCKLAND
IBADAN   NAIROBI   HARARE   GABORONE
SINGAPORE   TOKYO   PORTSMOUTH NH (USA)

ISBN 0 435 12287 8

92 93 94 95 14 13 12 11 10 9 8 7 6

Printed in England by Clays Ltd, St Ives plc

CONTENTS

Introduction	vi
The Withered Arm	1
The Son's Veto	34
Tony Kytes, the Arch-Deceiver	51
Absent-mindedness in a Parish Choir	61
The Melancholy Hussar of the German Legion	65
The Distracted Preacher	86

INTRODUCTION

Thomas Hardy lived from 1840 to 1928. During this long life he wrote fifteen novels (one of them unpublished) and about a thousand poems. He also published four volumes of short stories, from which this selection is taken.

He was born, and lived the greater part of his life, near Dorchester, the county town of Dorset. Most of what he wrote is set in Dorset and the neighbouring counties of Devon, Somerset, Cornwall, Hampshire, Wiltshire, Berkshire and Oxford. To this section of south-west England he gave the fictional name Wessex, called his first book of poetry 'Wessex Poems' and his first collection of short stories *Wessex Tales*. He even called his dog Wessex. Hardy borrowed the name from the general title by which this area of England had been known in Anglo-Saxon times, and through Hardy's work this name is generally now applied to the district.

The son of a small builder and mason, Hardy was born in a cottage which had been built for his grandfather, and was brought up there by his mother, father, and the grandfather's widow. It was an isolated building on the edge of a tract of wild heathland, for which Hardy, in one of his novels, invented the name Egdon Heath. The family – Hardy had two sisters and a brother – were thrown much together, yet each showed a certain pride and independence. They had to find their own forms of entertainment, and much of Hardy's boyhood was spent listening to the tales and traditions told by his father, mother and grandmother. Such stories form the basis of dozens of events, characters and incidents in his own works.

This is specially obvious in Hardy's short stories. Unlike novels, where the plot can unfold slowly and characters develop gradually, a short story needs to make its effect briefly and swiftly. There is no room for side-tracks, nor for remarks which do not carry the action forward. A short story resembles an anecdote of curious, gripping or interesting events, all leading to one dramatic point. Its ending must embody that point in vivid form, like a person bringing a spoken tale to an effective finish for a listening audience. Many of Hardy's short stories echo much that he must have heard round his own fireside, told to the family among themselves. Very often either the whole story or details in it can be traced to experiences known to the Hardy family or to some members of it. Frequently they embody, in one way or another, happenings known to Hardy when he was a boy, often repeated by his relatives, and stored up in his mind until the time in which he himself became a writer. The telling of such tales was a regular pastime in the small circle of the Hardy family, and as he grew up, he learned to shape them for a wider audience.

For instance, when Hardy was still a boy, he knew of an old woman who, to cure some wasting disease, had been taken in her youth to have her 'blood turned' by a convict's corpse, in the way he afterwards described in his story *The Withered Arm*. Trendle, the 'white wizard' or 'conjuror', who recommends this cure to Gertrude in the story, was a type of man familiar to Hardy as a boy, largely through his mother's stories about the experiences of her own relatives. One of these characters was a man known in his mother's own Dorset village as 'The Planet-Ruler' who seems to have been some kind of country astrologer or fortune-teller. One of Hardy's aunts consulted him about her future. Another similar man, known to Hardy or his mother, would help people who had been bewitched, and, so it was said, 'would cause your enemy to rise in a glass of water. He did not himself know your enemy's name, but the bewitched person did, of course, recognizing the form as one he had expected.'

Hardy makes use of this idea as well in *The Withered Arm*. Traditions of witches and witchcraft lasted a long time in the Dorset villages that Hardy knew, and went on until after his death. Within living memory, a village which he knew well, where several of his relatives lived, was supposed to have a witch who helped the local football team by putting an ill-luck curse on visiting opponents, so that the home team could never be beaten. Apart from such things, *The Withered Arm* is full of memories of Hardy's youth, including some of his own experiences. Even a tiny detail, such as the rustle made by the heroine's silk dress when she goes to church, was taken from an observation, in Hardy's own childhood, of the sound of the long gown of the Lady of the Manor as she made her way to her pew in the local church.

Thomas Hardy once told an admirer of his work that he himself thought *The Son's Veto* was his best short story. It is certainly one of the most bitter in its indignation and strong feeling against class distinction, prejudice and snobbery. When a widowed clergyman marries his parlourmaid, Hardy comments in this story that the vicar had 'committed social suicide'. All through the nineteenth century (the story appeared in 1891) for a middle-class person to marry his servant was reckoned to be a disgrace. Hardy was deeply conscious of this social taboo, since his own mother had been a servant to a Dorset vicar. Though she did not herself marry a middle-class man, there was an incident involving his mother during Hardy's own childhood, of which Hardy would have been well aware, and which would have given him an early insight into class prejudice.

As a child, Hardy was particularly favoured by the Lady of the Manor at the local mansion. She was childless, and showed special interest in Hardy, treating him almost like a child of her own, and inviting him to her grand house. This was resented by Hardy's mother, and, according to Hardy, she 'openly defied' the lady. No one knows what exactly happened, but it is certainly true that Hardy's mother took Hardy away from the village school, which the lady had founded, and sent him to a school in Dorchester. Hardy's mother had a strong will of her own, unlike the heroine of *The Son's Veto*, who allows her life to be ruled by the middle-class people her marriage has put her among, and, in the end, to be fatally frustrated by the snobbery of her own son. Hardy almost certainly inherited a touchiness about class differences, which he pours into the telling of this tragic little tale.

The short story, *Absent-mindedness in a Parish Choir*, where the band of musicians in the church gallery go to sleep during a service, and, waking up, think they are playing for a village dance, is made up almost entirely from incidents in Hardy's own childhood. From his grandfather's time, the Hardy family had been the mainstay of the small band that provided the music for the church, in the days before each church was provided with a small organ and organist for the music. His grandfather played the cello, his father, uncle, and a relative-in-law played violins. Hardy's mother described the band's appearance when they wore their best clothes for Sunday, a blue swallowtail coat with gilt buttons, red and black waistcoats, Wellington boots and French-blue trousers. His father also played for the country dances in village halls and neighbours' houses. Hardy himself learned how to tune a fiddle when very young, and to play hundreds of country dances from his father's and grandfather's old music books. When he was still a boy, his father, who was in great demand as a player, took Hardy to play with him at dances in the neighbouring villages. These occasions used to excite young Hardy beyond measure, and he became obsessed with playing. On one occasion he played a favourite tune, called 'The New-Rigged Ship', for three-quarters of an hour on end, and the hostess at the party had actually to seize hold of his bowing arm to make him stop, in case he did himself some injury in his excitement. Hardy's short story of the village band forgetting they were in church, losing their heads, and playing a dance-tune, clearly comes from the excitement over music he himself felt when he was a boy.

Thomas Hardy was also obsessed, from the time of his childhood, with the events of the long wars against Napoleon, which had taken place in the time of his grandfather. He found in a cupboard in the cottage a set of periodicals called *A History of the Wars*, to which his grandfather had subscribed because he himself had been a volunteer in the local militia, raised in the years 1804–1805, when, it was feared, Napoleon intended to invade England and land on the Dorset coast. Hardy wrote one full-length novel, *The Trumpet-Major*, and several short stories about the Napoleonic Wars, of which one, *The Melancholy Hussar*, is given in this book.

He was also intensely interested in Admiral Hardy, who had been Nelson's captain in his flagship, the *Victory*, which fought in the battle of Trafalgar in these wars. He liked to think that Captain Hardy, also a Dorset man, had some connection with his own family, though when asked about this, he had to confess there was no proof. However, this idea and the stories of the Hardy family combined to make the events of the wars against Napoleon a lifelong interest for Hardy, and after many schemes and sketches, including the novel and the short stories, he eventually produced, when in his sixties, a vast epic about these wars, which he called *The Dynasts*. This immense work, though in dramatic form, is more or less unactable, though it has many fine moments, and shortened versions have appeared, both during Hardy's own life and in modern times. Much of Hardy's material was gathered by research in the British Museum where he took notes, including details about the execution of deserters, which form part of *The Melancholy Hussar*. For Hardy, these events of a past age were as real as the happenings of his own time, and this gives an air of truth to the telling of such stories.

When he came to the story called *The Distracted Preacher*, Hardy had no difficulty in making the details of the smuggling realistic. 'My grandfather,' he once wrote, 'used to do a little in smuggling.' Though this grandfather had died just before Hardy was born, his widow, Hardy's grandmother, still lived with Hardy's parents, and did not die until he was seventeen. Hardy therefore knew her all through his schooldays, and no doubt she told him true stories of smuggling, which used to take place all along the south coast of England to evade the duty on such things as imported spirits. The Hardy house was a lonely one, about six miles inland from the coast, ideal for hiding smuggled tubs or barrels of brandy, landed by night from abroad, and brought to a hiding-place after dark. At two or three in the morning, Hardy said, the crack of a whip across one of the lower windows of the cottage would awake Hardy's grandfather. When he dressed and went downstairs, he would find no one there, but a pile of tubs outside the door. He hid these in a dark cupboard, and the following evening the smugglers would return and carry them away to sell to favoured customers. Hardy's grandmother objected, but the smugglers took no notice, and when one of Hardy's uncles was born, they even left a present of brandy specially for the christening. In the time of Hardy's own mother, the house was still visited by a woman smuggler selling brandy.

One of the men who worked for Hardy's father, the builder, had been a member of the smuggling gang, and told him many stories. It was he who told Hardy the device of hiding the smuggled goods in a pit, which was then concealed by an apple-tree planted in a tray or box, which could be lifted out by the gang coming to fetch the smuggled goods from their hiding-place. Hardy makes use of this true tale in his own story, *The Distracted Preacher*.

Apart from a few efforts for a local paper, and a joking sketch he wrote to amuse his fellow architectural students when he was in his twenties, Hardy did not write short stories for publication until the year 1874. In that year he had his first great success with a novel, *Far From the Madding Crowd*, and his name as a writer of fiction became known to editors. In the same year he married, also partly on the strength of the success of this novel, gave up the profession of architect, for which he had trained, and decided to depend on writing for a living. He therefore needed more money; short stories for magazines paid well, and were a useful way of supplementing his income from the novels, which he continued to write regularly.

Hardy has often been accused of being a pessimist, a label which he always refused to accept as being true. He saw life as full of ironic contrasts, and in fact he called one of his books of short stories by the title *Life's Little Ironies*; but he had a sly sense of humour and could tell an amusing story in a lively way. His tales *Tony Kytes the Arch-Deceiver* and *Absent-mindedness in a Parish Choir* demonstrate his gift for comedy. It is true that one tale in the present book ends with a hanging and another with two military deserters being shot; but Hardy would claim that such things do happen, and that it is the business of a writer to portray them truly. At his best, he keeps a balance between comedy and tragedy. In *The Distracted Preacher* he is fair to all characters, the smugglers and the government men who try to prevent the smuggling. There is suspense all through the story, but also a great deal of quiet humour, and, after their various troubles, all ends happily for the hero and heroine, in spite of the conflicts of their two ways of life.

Hardy believed that life had its difficulties, but that human beings were capable of overcoming these, and, with reasonable good will, of working out a satisfactory solution by which they could come to some measure of happiness. He believed that it was up to men and women themselves to make things better for the human race. The people in Hardy's stories are human beings with ordinary feelings, ambitions, faults and weaknesses. He seldom portrays out-of-the-way characters with anything special about them, though they may have occasional oddities. They are entirely believable, and their motives and the way they express themselves are simple. Although times may have changed – some of these stories were written a hundred years ago – the people and the situations he writes about are completely understandable today.

Robert Gittings

THE WITHERED ARM

I

IT was an eighty-cow dairy, and the troop of milkers, regular and supernumerary, were all at work; for, though the time of year was as yet but early April, the feed lay entirely in water-meadows, and the cows were 'in full pail'. The hour was about six in the evening, and three-fourths of the large, red, rectangular animals having been finished off, there was opportunity for a little conversation.

'He do bring home his bride to-morrow, I hear. They've come as far as Anglebury to-day.'

The voice seemed to proceed from the belly of the cow called Cherry, but the speaker was a milking-woman, whose face was buried in the flank of that motionless beast.

'Hav' anybody seen her?' said another.

There was a negative response from the first. 'Though they say she's a rosy-cheeked, tisty-tosty little body enough,' she added; and as the milkmaid spoke she turned her face so that she could glance past her cow's tail to the other side of the barton, where a thin fading woman of thirty milked somewhat apart from the rest.

'Years younger than he, they say,' continued the second, with also a glance of reflectiveness in the same direction.

'How old do you call him, then?'

'Thirty or so.'

'More like forty,' broke in an old milkman near, in a long white pinafore or 'wropper', and with the brim of his hat tied down, so that he looked like a woman. ''A was born before our Great Weir was builded, and I hadn't man's wages when I laved water there.'

The discussion waxed so warm that the purr of the milk

streams became jerky, till a voice from another cow's belly cried with authority, 'Now then, what the Turk do it matter to us about Farmer Lodge's age, or Farmer Lodge's new mis'ess? I shall have to pay him nine pound a year for the rent of every one of these milchers, whatever his age or hers. Get on with your work, or 'twill be dark afore we have done. The evening is pinking in a'ready.' This speaker was the dairyman himself, by whom the milkmaids and men were employed.

Nothing more was said publicly about Farmer Lodge's wedding, but the first woman murmured under her cow to her next neighbour. ''Tis hard for *she*,' signifying the thin worn milkmaid aforesaid.

'O no,' said the second. 'He ha'n't spoke to Rhoda Brook for years.'

When the milking was done they washed their pails and hung them on a many-forked stand made as usual of the peeled limb of an oak-tree, set upright in the earth, and resembling a colossal antlered horn. The majority then dispersed in various directions homeward. The thin woman who had not spoken was joined by a boy of twelve or thereabout, and the twain went away up the field also.

Their course lay apart from that of the others, to a lonely spot high above the water-meads, and not far from the border of Egdon Heath, whose dark countenance was visible in the distance as they drew nigh to their home.

'They've just been saying down in barton that your father brings his young wife home from Anglebury tomorrow,' the woman observed. 'I shall want to send you for a few things to market, and you'll be pretty sure to meet 'em.'

'Yes, mother,' said the boy. 'Is father married then?'

'Yes . . . You can give her a look, and tell me what she's like, if you do see her.'

'Yes, mother.'

'If she's dark or fair, and if she's tall – as tall as I. And if she seems like a woman who has ever worked for a living, or one that has been always well off, and has never done anything, and shows marks of the lady on her, as I expect she do.'

'Yes.'

They crept up the hill in the twilight and entered the cottage. It was built of mud-walls, the surface of which had been washed by many rains into channels and depressions that left none of the original flat face visible; while here and there in the thatch above a rafter showed like a bone protruding through the skin.

She was kneeling down in the chimney-corner, before two pieces of turf laid together with the heather inwards, blowing at the red-hot ashes with her breath till the turves flamed. The radiance lit her pale cheek, and made her dark eyes, that had once been handsome, seem handsome anew. 'Yes,' she resumed, 'see if she is dark or fair, and if you can, notice if her hands be white; if not, see if they look as though she had ever done housework, or are milker's hands like mine.'

The boy again promised, inattentively this time, his mother not observing that he was cutting a notch with his pocket-knife in the beech-backed chair.

THE YOUNG WIFE

II

The road from Anglebury to Holmstoke is in general level; but there is one place where a sharp ascent breaks its monotony. Farmers homeward-bound from the former market-town, who trot all the rest of the way, walk their horses up this short incline.

The next evening while the sun was yet bright a handsome new gig, with a lemon-coloured body and red wheels, was spinning westward along the level highway at the heels of a powerful mare. The driver was a yeoman in the prime of life, cleanly shaven like an actor, his face being toned to that bluish-vermilion hue which so often graces a thriving farmer's features when returning home after successful dealings in the town. Beside him sat a woman, many years his junior – almost, indeed, a girl. Her face too was fresh in colour, but it was of a totally different quality – soft and evanescent, like the light under a heap of rose-petals.

Few people travelled this way, for it was not a main road; and the long white riband of gravel that stretched before them was empty, save of one small scarce-moving speck, which presently resolved itself into the figure of a boy, who was creeping on at a snail's pace, and continually looking behind him – the heavy bundle he carried being some excuse for, if not the reason of, his dilatoriness. When the bouncing gig-party slowed at the bottom of the incline above mentioned, the pedestrian was only a few yards in front. Supporting the large bundle by putting one hand on his hip, he turned and looked straight at the farmer's wife as though he would read her through and through, pacing along abreast of the horse.

The low sun was full in her face, rendering every feature, shade, and contour distinct, from the curve of her little nostril to the colour of her eyes. The farmer, though he seemed annoyed at the boy's persistent presence, did not order him to get out of the way; and thus the lad preceded them, his hard gaze never leaving her, till they reached the top of the ascent, when the farmer trotted on with relief in his lineaments – having taken no outward notice of the boy whatever.

'How that poor lad stared at me!' said the young wife.

'Yes, dear; I saw that he did.'

'He is one of the village, I suppose?'

'One of the neighbourhood. I think he lives with his mother a mile or two off.'

'He knows who we are, no doubt?'

'O yes. You must expect to be stared at just at first, my pretty Gertrude.'

'I do, – though I think the poor boy may have looked at us in the hope we might relieve him of his heavy load, rather than from curiosity.'

'O no,' said her husband off-handedly. 'These country lads will carry a hundredweight once they get it on their backs; besides his pack had more size than weight in it. Now, then, another mile and I shall be able to show you our house in the distance – if it is not too dark before we get there.' The wheels spun round, and particles flew from their periphery as before, till a white house of ample dimensions revealed itself, with farm-buildings and ricks at the back.

Meanwhile the boy had quickened his pace, and turning up a by-lane some mile and half short of the white farm-stead, ascended towards the leaner pastures, and so on to the cottage of his mother.

She had reached home after her day's milking at the outlying dairy, and was washing cabbage at the doorway in the declining light. 'Hold up the net a moment,' she said, without preface, as the boy came up.

He flung down his bundle, held the edge of the cabbage-net, and as she filled its meshes with the dripping leaves she went on, 'Well, did you see her?'

'Yes; quite plain.'

'Is she ladylike?'

'Yes; and more. A lady complete.'

'Is she young?'

'Well, she's growed up, and her ways be quite a woman's.'

'Of course. What colour is her hair and face?'

'Her hair is lightish, and her face as comely as a live doll's.'

'Her eyes, then, are not dark like mine?'

'No – of a bluish turn, and her mouth is very nice and

red; and when she smiles, her teeth show white.'

'Is she tall?' said the woman sharply.

'I couldn't see. She was sitting down.'

'Then do you go to Holmstoke church to-morrow morning: she's sure to be there. Go early and notice her walking in, and come home and tell me if she's taller than I.'

'Very well, mother. But why don't you go and see for yourself?'

'*I* go to see her! I wouldn't look up at her if she were to pass my window this instant. She was with Mr Lodge, of course. What did he say or do?'

'Just the same as usual.'

'Took no notice of you?'

'None.'

Next day the mother put a clean shirt on the boy, and started him off for Holmstoke church. He reached the ancient little pile when the door was just being opened, and he was the first to enter. Taking his seat by the font, he watched all the parishioners file in. The well-to-do Farmer Lodge came nearly last; and his young wife, who accompanied him, walked up the aisle with the shyness natural to a modest woman who had appeared thus for the first time. As all other eyes were fixed upon her, the youth's stare was not noticed now.

When he reached home his mother said, 'Well?' before he had entered the room.

'She is not tall. She is rather short,' he replied.

'Ah!' said his mother, with satisfaction.

'But she's very pretty – very. In fact, she's lovely.' The youthful freshness of the yeoman's wife had evidently made an impression even on the somewhat hard nature of the boy.

'That's all I want to hear,' said his mother quickly. 'Now, spread the table-cloth. The hare you wired is very tender; but mind that nobody catches you. – You've never told me what sort of hands she had.'

'I have never seen 'em. She never took off her gloves.'

'What did she wear this morning?'

'A white bonnet and a silver-coloured gownd. It whewed and whistled so loud when it rubbed against the pews that the lady coloured up more than ever for very shame at the noise, and pulled it in to keep it from touching; but when she pushed into her seat, it whewed more than ever. Mr Lodge, he seemed pleased, and his waistcoat stuck out, and his great golden seals hung like a lord's; but she seemed to wish her noisy gownd anywhere but on her.'

'Not she! However, that will do now.'

These descriptions of the newly-married couple were continued from time to time by the boy at his mother's request, after any chance encounter he had had with them. But Rhoda Brook, though she might easily have seen young Mrs Lodge for herself by walking a couple of miles, would never attempt an excursion towards the quarter where the farmhouse lay. Neither did she, at the daily milking in the dairyman's yard on Lodge's outlying second farm, ever speak on the subject of the recent marriage. The dairyman who rented the cows of Lodge, and knew perfectly the tall milkmaid's history, with manly kindliness always kept the gossip in the cow-barton from annoying Rhoda. But the atmosphere thereabout was full of the subject during the first days of Mrs Lodge's arrival; and from her boy's description and the casual words of the other milkers, Rhoda Brook could raise a mental image of the unconscious Mrs Lodge that was realistic as a photograph.

A VISION

III

One night, two or three weeks after the bridal return, when the boy was gone to bed, Rhoda sat a long time over the turf ashes that she had raked out in front of her to extinguish them. She contemplated so intently the new wife, as presented to her in her mind's eye over the embers, that she forgot the lapse of time. At last, wearied with her day's work, she too retired.

But the figure which had occupied her so much during this and the previous days was not to be banished at night. For the first time Gertrude Lodge visited the supplanted woman in her dreams. Rhoda Brook dreamed – since her assertion that she really saw, before falling asleep, was not to be believed – that the young wife, in the pale silk dress and white bonnet, but with features shockingly distorted, and wrinkled as by age, was sitting upon her chest as she lay. The pressure of Mrs Lodge's person grew heavier; the blue eyes peered cruelly into her face; and then the figure thrust forward its left hand mockingly, so as to make the wedding-ring it wore glitter in Rhoda's eyes. Maddened mentally, and nearly suffocated by pressure, the sleeper struggled; the incubus, still regarding her, withdrew to the foot of the bed, only, however, to come forward by degrees, resume her seat, and flash her left hand as before.

Gasping for breath, Rhoda, in a last desperate effort, swung out her right hand, seized the confronting spectre by its obtrusive left arm, and whirled it backward to the floor, starting up herself as she did so with a low cry.

'O, merciful heaven!' she cried, sitting on the edge of the bed in a cold sweat; 'that was not a dream – she was here!'

She could feel her antagonist's arm within her grasp even now – the very flesh and bone of it, as it seemed. She looked on the floor whither she had whirled the spectre, but there was nothing to be seen.

Rhoda Brook slept no more that night, and when she went milking at the next dawn they noticed how pale and haggard she looked. The milk that she drew quivered into the pail; her hand had not calmed even yet, and still retained the feel of the arm. She came home to breakfast as wearily as if it had been supper-time.

'What was that noise in your chimmer, mother, last night?' said her son. 'You fell off the bed, surely?'

'Did you hear anything fall? At what time?'

'Just when the clock struck two.'

She could not explain, and when the meal was done went silently about her household work, the boy assisting her, for he hated going afield on the farms, and she indulged his reluctance. Between eleven and twelve the garden-gate clicked, and she lifted her eyes to the window. At the bottom of the garden, within the gate, stood the woman of her vision. Rhoda seemed transfixed.

'Ah, she said she would come!' exclaimed the boy, also observing her.

'Said so – when? How does she know us?'

'I have seen and spoken to her. I talked to her yesterday.'

'I told you,' said the mother, flushing indignantly, 'never to speak to anybody in that house, or go near the place.'

'I did not speak to her till she spoke to me. And I did not go near the place. I met her in the road.'

'What did you tell her?'

'Nothing. She said, ''Are you the poor boy who had to bring the heavy load from market?'' And she looked at my boots, and said they would not keep my feet dry if it came on wet, because they were so cracked. I told her I lived with my mother, and we had enough to do to keep ourselves, and that's how it was; and she said then, ''I'll come and bring you some better boots, and see your mother.'' She gives away things to other folks in the meads besides us.'

Mrs Lodge was by this time close to the door – not in her silk, as Rhoda had dreamt of in the bedchamber, but in a morning hat, and gown of common light material, which became her better than silk. On her arm she carried a basket.

The impression remaining from the night's experience was still strong. Brook had almost expected to see the wrinkles, the scorn, and the cruelty on her visitor's face. She would have escaped an interview, had escape been possible. There was, however, no backdoor to the cottage, and in an instant the boy had lifted the latch to Mrs Lodge's gentle knock.

'I see I have come to the right house,' said she, glancing at the lad, and smiling. 'But I was not sure till you opened the door.'

The figure and action were those of the phantom; but her voice was so indescribably sweet, her glance so winning, her smile so tender, so unlike that of Rhoda's midnight visitant, that the latter could hardly believe the evidence of her senses. She was truly glad that she had not hidden away in sheer aversion, as she had been inclined to do. In her basket Mrs Lodge brought the pair of boots that she had promised to the boy, and other useful articles.

At these proofs of a kindly feeling towards her and hers Rhoda's heart reproached her bitterly. This innocent young thing should have her blessing and not her curse. When she left them a light seemed gone from the dwelling. Two days later she came again to know if the boots fitted; and less than a fortnight after that paid Rhoda another call. On this occasion the boy was absent.

'I walk a good deal,' said Mrs Lodge, 'and your house is the nearest outside our own parish. I hope you are well. You don't look quite well.'

Rhoda said she was well enough; and, indeed, though the paler of the two, there was more of the strength that endures in her well-defined features and large frame than in the soft-cheeked young woman before her. The conversation became quite confidential as regarded their powers and weaknesses; and when Mrs Lodge was leaving, Rhoda said, 'I hope you will find this air agree with you, ma'am, and not suffer from the damp of the water meads.'

The younger one replied that there was not much doubt of it, her general health being usually good. 'Though, now you remind me,' she added, 'I have one little ailment which puzzles me. It is nothing serious, but I cannot make it out.'

She uncovered her left hand and arm; and their outline confronted Rhoda's gaze as the exact original of the limb she had beheld and seized in her dream. Upon the pink round surface of the arm were faint marks of an unhealthy colour, as if produced by a rough grasp. Rhoda's eyes became riveted on the discolorations; she fancied that she discerned in them the shape of her own four fingers.

'How did it happen?' she said mechanically.

'I cannot tell,' replied Mrs Lodge, shaking her head. 'One night when I was sound asleep, dreaming I was away in some strange place, a pain suddenly shot into my arm there, and was so keen as to awaken me. I must have struck it in the daytime, I suppose, though I don't remember doing so.' She added, laughing, 'I tell my dear husband that it looks just as if he had flown into a rage and struck me there. O, I daresay it will soon disappear.'

'Ha, ha! Yes . . . On what night did it come?'

Mrs Lodge considered, and said it would be a fortnight ago on the morrow. 'When I awoke I could not remember where I was,' she added, 'till the clock striking two reminded me.'

She had named the night and the hour of Rhoda's spectral encounter, and Brook felt like a guilty thing. The artless disclosure startled her; she did not reason on the freaks of coincidence; and all the scenery of that ghastly night returned with double vividness to her mind.

'O, can it be,' she said to herself, when her visitor had departed, 'that I exercise a malignant power over people against my own will?' She knew that she had been slyly called a witch since her fall; but never having understood why that particular stigma had been attached to her, it had passed disregarded. Could this be the explanation, and had such things as this ever happened before?

A SUGGESTION

IV

The summer drew on, and Rhoda Brook almost dreaded to meet Mrs Lodge again, notwithstanding that her feeling for the young wife amounted well-nigh to affection. Something in her own individuality seemed to convict Rhoda of crime. Yet a fatality sometimes would direct the steps of the latter to the outskirts of Holmstoke whenever she left her house for any other purpose than her daily work; and hence it happened that their next encounter was out of doors. Rhoda could not avoid the subject which had so mystified her, and after the first few words she stammered, 'I hope your – arm is well again, ma'am?' She had perceived with consternation that Gertrude Lodge carried her left arm stiffly.

'No; it is not quite well. Indeed it is no better at all; it is rather worse. It pains me dreadfully sometimes.'

'Perhaps you had better go to a doctor, ma'am.'

She replied that she had already seen a doctor. Her husband had insisted upon her going to one. But the surgeon had not seemed to understand the afflicted limb at all; he had told her to bathe it in hot water, and she had bathed it, but the treatment had done no good.

'Will you let me see it?' said the milkwoman.

Mrs Lodge pushed up her sleeve and disclosed the place, which was a few inches above the wrist. As soon as Rhoda Brook saw it, she could hardly preserve her composure. There was nothing of the nature of a wound, but the arm at that point had a shrivelled look, and the outline of the four fingers appeared more distinct than at the former time. Moreover, she fancied that they were imprinted in precisely the relative position of her clutch upon the arm in the trance; the first finger towards Gertrude's wrist, and the fourth towards her elbow.

What the impress resembled seemed to have struck Gertrude herself since their last meeting. 'It looks almost like fingermarks,' she said; adding with a faint laugh, 'my husband says it is as if some witch, or the devil himself, had taken hold of me there, and blasted the flesh.'

Rhoda shivered. 'That's fancy,' she said hurriedly. 'I wouldn't mind it, if I were you.'

'I shouldn't so much mind it,' said the younger, with hesitation, 'if – if I hadn't a notion that it makes my husband – dislike me – no, love me less. Men think so much of personal appearance.'

'Some do – he for one.'

'Yes; and he was very proud of mine, at first.'

'Keep your arm covered from his sight.'

'Ah – he knows the disfigurement is there!' She tried to hide the tears that filled her eyes.

'Well, ma'am, I earnestly hope it will go away soon.'

And so the milkwoman's mind was chained anew to the subject by a horrid sort of spell as she returned home. The sense of having been guilty of an act of malignity increased, affect as she might to ridicule her superstition. In her secret heart Rhoda did not altogether object to a slight diminution of her successor's beauty, by whatever means it had come about; but she did not wish to inflict upon her physical pain. For though this pretty young woman had rendered impossible any reparation which Lodge might have made Rhoda for his past conduct, everything like resentment at the unconscious usurpation had quite passed away from the elder's mind.

If the sweet and kindly Gertrude Lodge only knew of the dream-scene in the bed-chamber, what would she think? Not to inform her of it seemed treachery in the presence of her friendliness; but tell she could not of her own accord – neither could she devise a remedy.

She mused upon the matter the greater part of the night; and the next day, after the morning milking, set out to obtain another glimpse of Gertrude Lodge if she could, being held to her by a gruesome fascination. By watching the house from a distance the milkmaid was presently able to discern the farmer's wife in a ride she was taking alone – probably to join her husband in some distant field. Mrs Lodge perceived her, and cantered in her direction.

'Good morning, Rhoda!' Gertrude said, when she had come up. 'I was going to call.'

Rhoda noticed that Mrs Lodge held the reins with some difficulty.

'I hope – the bad arm,' said Rhoda.

'They tell me there is possibly one way by which I might be able to find out the cause, and so perhaps the cure, of it,' replied the other anxiously. 'It is by going to some clever man over in Egdon Heath. They did not know if he was still alive – and I cannot remember his name at this moment; but they said that you knew more of his movements than anybody else hereabout, and could tell me if he were still to be consulted. Dear me – what was his name? But you know.'

'Not Conjuror Trendle?' said her thin companion, turning pale.

'Trendle – yes. Is he alive?'

'I believe so,' said Rhoda with reluctance.

'Why do you call him conjuror?'

'Well – they say – they used to say he was a – he had powers other folks have not.'

'O, how could my people be so superstitious as to recommend a man of that sort! I thought they meant some medical man. I shall think no more of him.'

Rhoda looked relieved, and Mrs Lodge rode on. The milkwoman had inwardly seen, from the moment she heard of her having been mentioned as a reference for this man, that there must exist a sarcastic feeling among the work-folk that a sorceress would know the whereabouts of the exorcist. They suspected her, then. A short time ago this would have given no concern to a woman of her common-sense. But she had a haunting reason to be superstitious now; and she had

been seized with sudden dread that this Conjuror Trendle
might name her as the malignant influence which was
blasting the fair person of Gertrude, and so lead her friend
to hate her for ever, and to treat her as some fiend in human
shape.

But all was not over. Two days after, a shadow intruded
into the window-pattern thrown on Rhoda Brook's floor by
the afternoon sun. The woman opened the door at once,
almost breathlessly.

'Are you alone?' said Gertrude. She seemed to be no less
harassed and anxious than Brook herself.

'Yes,' said Rhoda.

'The place on my arm seems worse, and troubles me!' the
young farmer's wife went on. 'It is so mysterious! I do hope
it will not be an incurable wound. I have again been
thinking of what they said about Conjuror Trendle. I don't
really believe in such men, but I should not mind just
visiting him, from curiosity – though on no account must
my husband know. Is it far to where he lives?'

'Yes – five miles,' said Rhoda backwardly. 'In the heart
of Egdon.'

'Well, I should have to walk. Could not you go with me to
show me the way – say to-morrow afternoon?'

'O, not I; that is –,' the milkwoman murmured, with a
start of dismay. Again the dread seized her that something
to do with her fierce act in the dream might be revealed, and
her character in the eyes of the most useful friend she had
ever had be ruined irretrievably.

Mrs Lodge urged, and Rhoda finally assented, though
with much misgiving. Sad as the journey would be to her,
she could not conscientiously stand in the way of a possible
remedy for her patron's strange affliction. It was agreed
that, to escape suspicion of their mystic intent, they should
meet at the edge of the heath at the corner of a plantation
which was visible from the spot where they now stood.

CONJUROR TRENDLE

V

By the next afternoon Rhoda would have done anything to
escape this inquiry. But she had promised to go. Moreover,
there was a horrid fascination at times in becoming instru-
mental in throwing such possible light on her own character
as would reveal her to be something greater in the occult
world than she had ever herself suspected.

She started just before the time of day mentioned
between them, and half-an-hour's brisk walking brought
her to the south-eastern extension of the Egdon tract of
country, where the fir plantation was. A slight figure,
cloaked and veiled, was already there. Rhoda recognized,
almost with a shudder, that Mrs Lodge bore her left arm in
a sling.

They hardly spoke to each other, and immediately set out
on their climb into the interior of this solemn country,
which stood high above the rich alluvial soil they had left
half-an-hour before. It was a long walk; thick clouds made
the atmosphere dark, though it was as yet only early afternoon; and the wind howled dismally over the slopes of the
heath – not improbably the same heath which had witnessed
the agony of the Wessex King Ina, presented to after-ages as
Lear. Gertrude Lodge talked most, Rhoda replying with
monosyllabic preoccupation. She had a strange dislike to
walking on the side of her companion where hung the
afflicted arm, moving round to the other when inadver-
tently near it. Much heather had been brushed by their feet
when they descended upon a cart-track, beside which stood
the house of the man they sought.

He did not profess his remedial practices openly, or care
anything about their continuance, his direct interests being
those of a dealer in furze, turf, 'sharp sand', and other local
products. Indeed, he affected not to believe largely in his
own powers, and when warts that had been shown him for

cure miraculously disappeared – which it must be owned they infallibly did – he would say lightly, 'O, I only drink a glass of grog upon 'em at your expense – perhaps it's all chance,' and immediately turn the subject.

He was at home when they arrived, having in fact seen them descending into his valley. He was a grey-bearded man, with a reddish face, and he looked singularly at Rhoda the first moment he beheld her. Mrs Lodge told him her errand; and then with words of self-disparagement he examined her arm.

'Medicine can't cure it,' he said promptly. ' 'Tis the work of an enemy.'

Rhoda shrank into herself, and drew back.

'An enemy? What enemy?' asked Mrs Lodge.

He shook his head. 'That's best known to yourself,' he said. 'If you like, I can show the person to you, though I shall not myself know who it is. I can do no more; and don't wish to do that.'

She pressed him; on which he told Rhoda to wait outside where she stood, and took Mrs Lodge into the room. It opened immediately from the door; and, as the latter remained ajar, Rhoda Brook could see the proceedings without taking part in them. He brought a tumbler from the dresser, nearly filled it with water, and fetching an egg, pre- pared it in some private way; after which he broke it on the edge of the glass, so that the white went in and the yolk remained. As it was getting gloomy, he took the glass and its contents to the window, and told Gertrude to watch the mixture closely. They leant over the table together, and the milkwoman could see the opaline hue of the egg-fluid changing form as it sank in the water, but she was not near enough to define the shape that it assumed.

'Do you catch the likeness of any face or figure as you look?' demanded the conjuror of the young woman.

She murmured a reply, in tones so low as to be inaudible to Rhoda, and continued to gaze intently into the glass.

Rhoda turned, and walked a few steps away.

When Mrs Lodge came out, and her face was met by the light, it appeared exceedingly pale – as pale as Rhoda's – against the sad dun shades of the upland's garniture. Trendle shut the door behind her, and they at once started homeward together. But Rhoda perceived that her companion had quite changed.

'Did he charge much?' she asked tentatively.

'O no – nothing. He would not take a farthing,' said Gertrude.

'And what did you see?' inquired Rhoda.

'Nothing I – care to speak of.' The constraint in her manner was remarkable; her face was so rigid as to wear an oldened aspect, faintly suggestive of the face in Rhoda's bed-chamber.

'Was it you who first proposed coming here?' Mrs Lodge suddenly inquired, after a long pause. 'How very odd, if you did!'

'No. But I am not sorry we have come, all things considered,' she replied. For the first time a sense of triumph possessed her, and she did not altogether deplore that the young thing at her side should learn that their lives had been antagonized by other influences than their own.

The subject was no more alluded to during the long and dreary walk home. But in some way or other a story was whispered about the main-dairied lowland that winter that Mrs Lodge's gradual loss of the use of her left arm was owing to her being 'overlooked' by Rhoda Brook. The latter kept her own counsel about the incubus, but her face grew sadder and thinner; and in the spring she and her boy disappeared from the neighbourhood of Holmstoke.

A SECOND ATTEMPT

VI

Half a dozen years passed away, and Mr and Mrs Lodge's married experience sank into prosiness, and worse. The farmer was usually gloomy and silent: the woman whom he had wooed for her grace and beauty was contorted and disfigured in the left limb; moreover, she had brought him no child, which rendered it likely that he would be the last of a family who had occupied that valley for some two hundred years. He thought of Rhoda Brook and her son; and feared this might be a judgement from heaven upon him.

The once blithe-hearted and enlightened Gertrude was changing into an irritable, superstitious woman, whose whole time was given to experimenting upon her ailment with every quack remedy she came across. She was honestly attached to her husband, and was ever secretly hoping against hope to win back his heart again by regaining some at least of her personal beauty. Hence it arose that her closet was lined with bottles, packets, and ointment-pots of every description – nay, bunches of mystic herbs, charms, and books of necromancy, which in her schoolgirl time she would have ridiculed as folly.

'Damned if you won't poison yourself with these apothecary messes and witch mixtures some time or other,' said her husband, when his eye chanced to fall upon the multitudinous array.

She did not reply, but turned her sad, soft glance upon him in such heart-swollen reproach that he looked sorry for his words, and added, 'I only meant it for your good, you know, Gertrude.'

'I'll clear out the whole lot, and destroy them,' said she huskily, 'and try such remedies no more!'

'You want somebody to cheer you,' he observed. 'I once thought of adopting a boy; but he is too old now. And he is gone away I don't know where.'

She guessed to whom he alluded; for Rhoda Brook's story had in the course of years become known to her; though not a word had ever passed between her husband and herself on the subject. Neither had she ever spoken to him of her visit to Conjuror Trendle, and of what was revealed to her, or she thought was revealed to her, by that solitary heathman.

She was now five-and-twenty; but she seemed older. 'Six years of marriage, and only a few months of love,' she sometimes whispered to herself. And then she thought of the apparent cause, and said, with a tragic glance at her withering limb, 'If I could only again be as I was when he first saw me!'

She obediently destroyed her nostrums and charms; but there remained a hankering wish to try something else – some other sort of cure altogether. She had never revisited Trendle since she had been conducted to the house of the solitary by Rhoda against her will; but it now suddenly occurred to Gertrude that she would, in a last desperate effort at deliverance from this seeming curse, again seek out the man, if he yet lived. He was entitled to a certain credence, for the indistinct form he had raised in the glass had undoubtedly resembled the only woman in the world who – as she now knew, though not then – could have a reason for bearing her ill-will. The visit should be paid.

This time she went alone, though she nearly got lost on the heath, and roamed a considerable distance out of her way. Trendle's house was reached at last, however: he was not indoors, and instead of waiting at the cottage, she went to where his bent figure was pointed out to her at work a long way off. Trendle remembered her, and laying down the handful of furze-roots which he was gathering and throwing into a heap, he offered to accompany her in her homeward direction, as the distance was considerable and the days were short. So they walked together, his head bowed nearly to the earth, and his form of a colour with it.

'You can send away warts and other excrescences, I know,' she said; 'why can't you send away this?' And the arm was uncovered.

'You think too much of my powers!' said Trendle; 'and I am old and weak now, too. No, no; it is too much for me to attempt in my own person. What have ye tried?'

She named to him some of the hundred medicaments and counterspells which she had adopted from time to time. He shook his head.

'Some were good enough,' he said approvingly; 'but not many of them for such as this. This is of the nature of a blight, not of the nature of a wound; and if you ever do throw it off, it will be all at once.'

'If I only could!'

'There is only one chance of doing it known to me. It has never failed in kindred afflictions, – that I can declare. But it is hard to carry out, and especially for a woman.'

'Tell me!' said she.

'You must touch with the limb the neck of a man who's been hanged.'

She started a little at the image he had raised.

'Before he's cold – just after he's cut down,' continued the conjuror impassively.

'How can that do good?'

'It will turn the blood and change the constitution. But, as I say, to do it is hard. You must go to the jail when there's a hanging, and wait for him when he's brought off the gallows. Lots have done it, though perhaps not such pretty women as you. I used to send dozens for skin complaints. But that was in former times. The last I sent was in '13 – near twelve years ago.'

He had no more to tell her; and, when he had put her into a straight track homeward, turned and left her, refusing all money as at first.

A RIDE

VII

The communication sank deep into Gertrude's mind. Her nature was rather a timid one; and probably of all remedies that the white wizard could have suggested there was not one which would have filled her with so much aversion as this, not to speak of the immense obstacles in the way of its adoption.

Casterbridge, the county-town, was a dozen or fifteen miles off; and though in those days, when men were executed for horse-stealing, arson, and burglary, an assize seldom passed without a hanging, it was not likely that she could get access to the body of the criminal unaided. And the fear of her husband's anger made her reluctant to breathe a word of Trendle's suggestion to him or to anybody about him.

She did nothing for months, and patiently bore her disfigurement as before. But her woman's nature, craving for renewed love, through the medium of renewed beauty (she was but twenty-five), was ever stimulating her to try what, at any rate, could hardly do her any harm. 'What came by a spell will go by a spell surely,' she would say. Whenever her imagination pictured the act she shrank in terror from the possibility of it: then the words of the conjuror, 'It will turn your blood', were seen to be capable of a scientific no less than a ghastly interpretation; the mastering desire returned, and urged her on again.

There was at this time but one county paper, and that her husband only occasionally borrowed. But old-fashioned days had old-fashioned means, and news was extensively conveyed by word of mouth from market to market, or from fair to fair, so that, whenever such an event as an execution was about to take place, few within a radius of twenty miles were ignorant of the coming sight; and, so far as Holmstoke was concerned, some enthusiasts had been known to walk all the way to Casterbridge and back in one day, solely to witness the spectacle. The next assizes were in March; and when Gertrude Lodge heard that they had been held, she inquired stealthily at the inn as to the result, as soon as she could find opportunity.

She was, however, too late. The time at which the sentences were to be carried out had arrived, and to make the journey and obtain admission at such short notice required at least her husband's assistance. She dared not tell him, for she had found by delicate experiment that these smouldering village beliefs made him furious if mentioned, partly because he half entertained them himself. It was therefore necessary to wait for another opportunity.

Her determination received a fillip from learning that two epileptic children had attended from this very village of Holmstoke many years before with beneficial results, though the experiment had been strongly condemned by the neighbouring clergy. April, May, June, passed; and it is no overstatement to say that by the end of the last-named month Gertrude well-nigh longed for the death of a fellow-creature. Instead of her formal prayers each night, her unconscious prayer was, 'O Lord, hang some guilty or innocent person soon!'

This time she made earlier inquiries, and was altogether more systematic in her proceedings. Moreover, the season was summer, between the haymaking and the harvest, and in the leisure thus afforded him her husband had been holi-day-taking away from home.

The assizes were in July, and she went to the inn as before. There was to be one execution – only one – for arson.

Her greatest problem was not how to get to Casterbridge, but what means she should adopt for obtaining admission to the jail. Though access for such purposes had formerly never been denied, the custom had fallen into desuetude; and in contemplating her possible difficulties, she was again almost driven to fall back upon her husband. But, on sounding him about the assizes, he was so uncommunicative, so more than usually cold, that she did not proceed, and decided that whatever she did she would do alone.

Fortune, obdurate hitherto, showed her unexpected favour. On the Thursday before the Saturday fixed for the execution, Lodge remarked to her that he was going away from home for another day or two on business at a fair, and that he was sorry he could not take her with him.

She exhibited on this occasion so much readiness to stay at home that he looked at her in surprise. Time had been when she would have shown deep disappointment at the loss of such a jaunt. However, he lapsed into his usual taciturnity, and on the day named left Holmstoke.

It was now her turn. She at first had thought of driving, but on reflection held that driving would not do, since it would necessitate her keeping to the turnpike-road, and so increase by tenfold the risk of her ghastly errand being found out. She decided to ride, and avoid the beaten track, notwithstanding that in her husband's stables there was no animal just at present which by any stretch of imagination could be considered a lady's mount, in spite of his promise before marriage to always keep a mare for her. He had, however, many cart-horses, fine ones of their kind; and among the rest was a serviceable creature, an equine Amazon, with a back as broad as a sofa, on which Gertrude had occasionally taken an airing when unwell. This horse she chose.

On Friday afternoon one of the men brought it round. She was dressed, and before going down looked at her shrivelled arm. 'Ah! she said to it, 'if it had not been for you this terrible ordeal would have been saved me!'

When strapping up the bundle in which she carried a few articles of clothing, she took occasion to say to the servant, 'I take these in case I should not get back to-night from the person I am going to visit. Don't be alarmed if I am not in by ten, and close up the house as usual. I shall be at home to-morrow for certain.' She meant then to tell her husband privately: the deed accomplished was not like the deed projected. He would almost certainly forgive her.

And then the pretty palpitating Gertrude Lodge went from her husband's homestead; but though her goal was Casterbridge she did not take the direct route thither through Stickleford. Her cunning course at first was in precisely the opposite direction. As soon as she was out of sight, however, she turned to the left, by a road which led into Egdon, and on entering the heath wheeled round, and set out in the true course, due westerly. A more private way down the county could not be imagined; and as to direction, she had merely to keep her horse's head to a point a little to the right of the sun. She knew that she would light upon a furze-cutter or cottager of some sort from time to time, from whom she might correct her bearing.

Though the date was comparatively recent, Egdon was much less fragmentary in character than now. The attempts – successful and otherwise – at cultivation on the lower slopes, which intrude and break up the original heath into small detached heaths, had not been carried far; Enclosure Acts had not taken effect, and the banks and fences which now exclude the cattle of those villagers who formerly enjoyed rights of commonage thereon, and the carts of those who had turbary privileges which kept them in firing all the year round, were not erected. Gertrude, therefore, rode along with no other obstacles than the prickly furze-bushes, the mats of heather, the white water-courses, and the natural steeps and declivities of the ground.

Her horse was sure, if heavy-footed and slow, and though a draught animal, was easy-paced; had it been otherwise, she was not a woman who could have ventured to ride over such a bit of country with a half-dead arm. It was therefore nearly eight o'clock when she drew rein to breathe her bearer on the last outlying high point of heath-land towards

Casterbridge, previous to leaving Egdon for the cultivated valleys.

She halted before a pool called Rushy-pond, flanked by the ends of two hedges; a railing ran through the centre of the pond, dividing it in half. Over the railing she saw the low green country; over the green trees the roofs of the town; over the roofs a white flat façade, denoting the entrance to the county jail. On the roof of this front specks were moving about; they seemed to be workmen erecting something. Her flesh crept. She descended slowly, and was soon amid corn-fields and pastures. In another half-hour, when it was almost dusk, Gertrude reached the White Hart, the first inn of the town on that side.

Little surprise was excited by her arrival; farmers' wives rode on horseback then more than they do now; though, for that matter, Mrs Lodge was not imagined to be a wife at all; the innkeeper supposed her some harum-skarum young woman who had come to attend 'hang-fair' next day. Neither her husband nor herself ever dealt in Casterbridge market, so that she was unknown. While dismounting she beheld a crowd of boys standing at the door of a harness-maker's shop just above the inn, looking inside it with deep interest.

'What is going on there?' she asked of the ostler.

'Making the rope for to-morrow.'

She throbbed responsively, and contracted her arm.

' 'Tis sold by the inch afterwards,' the man continued. 'I could get you a bit, miss, for nothing, if you'd like?'

She hastily repudiated any such wish, all the more from a curious creeping feeling that the condemned wretch's destiny was becoming interwoven with her own; and having engaged a room for the night, sat down to think.

Up to this time she had formed but the vaguest notions about her means of obtaining access to the prison. The words of the cunning-man returned to her mind. He had implied that she should use her beauty, impaired though it was, as a pass-key. In her inexperience she knew little about jail functionaries; she had heard of a high-sheriff and an under-sheriff, but dimly only. She knew, however, that there must be a hangman, and to the hangman she determined to apply.

A WATER-SIDE HERMIT

VIII

At this date, and for several years after, there was a hangman to almost every jail. Gertrude found, on inquiry, that the Casterbridge official dwelt in a lonely cottage by a deep slow river flowing under the cliff on which the prison buildings were situate – the stream being the self-same one, though she did not know it, which watered the Stickleford and Holmstoke meads lower down in its course.

Having changed her dress, and before she had eaten or drunk – for she could not take her ease till she had ascertained some particulars – Gertrude pursued her way by a path along the water-side to the cottage indicated. Passing thus the outskirts of the jail, she discerned on the level roof over the gateway three rectangular lines against the sky, where the specks had been moving in her distant view; she recognized what the erection was, and passed quickly on. Another hundred yards brought her to the executioner's house, which a boy pointed out. It stood close to the same stream, and was hard by a weir, the waters of which emitted a steady roar.

While she stood hesitating the door opened, and an old man came forth shading a candle with one hand. Locking the door on the outside, he turned to a flight of wooden steps fixed against the end of the cottage, and began to ascend them, this being evidently their staircase to his bedroom. Gertrude hastened forward, but by the time she reached the foot of the ladder he was at the top. She called to him loudly enough to be heard above the roar of the weir; he looked down and said, 'What d'ye want here?'

'To speak to you a minute.'

The candle-light, such as it was, fell upon her imploring, pale, upturned face, and Davies (as the hangman was called) backed down the ladder. 'I was just going to bed,' he said; ' "Early to bed and early to rise," but I don't mind stopping a minute for such a one as you. Come into house.' He reopened the door, and preceded her to the room within.

The implements of his daily work, which was that of a jobbing gardener, stood in a corner, and seeing probably that she looked rural, he said, 'If you want me to undertake country work I can't come, for I never leave Casterbridge for gentle nor simple – not I. My real calling is officer of justice,' he added formally.

'Yes, yes! That's it. To-morrow!'

'Ah! I thought so. Well, what's the matter about that? 'Tis no use to come here about the knot – folks do come continually, but I tell 'em one knot is as merciful as another if ye keep it under the ear. Is the unfortunate man a relation; or, I should say, perhaps' (looking at her dress) 'a person who's been in your employ?'

'No. What time is the execution?'

'The same as usual – twelve o'clock, or as soon after as the London mail-coach gets in. We always wait for that, in case of a reprieve.'

'O – a reprieve – I hope not!' she said involuntarily.

'Well, – hee, hee! – as a matter of business, so do I! But still, if ever a young fellow deserved to be let off, this one does; only just turned eighteen, and only present by chance when the rick was fired. Howsomever, there's not much risk of it, as they are obliged to make an example of him, there having been so much destruction of property that way lately.'

'I mean,' she explained, 'that I want to touch him for a

charm, a cure of an affliction, by the advice of a man who has proved the virtue of the remedy.'

'O yes, miss! Now I understand. I've had such people come in past years. But it didn't strike me that you looked of a sort to require blood-turning. What's the complaint? The wrong kind for this, I'll be bound.'

'My arm.' She reluctantly showed the withered skin.

'Ah! - 'tis all a-scram!' said the hangman, examining it.

'Yes,' said she.

'Well,' he continued, with interest, 'that *is* the class o' subject, I'm bound to admit! I like the look of the wownd; it is truly as suitable for the cure as any I ever saw. 'Twas a knowing-man that sent 'ee, whoever he was.'

'You can contrive for me all that's necessary?' she said breathlessly.

'You should really have gone to the governor of the jail, and your doctor with 'ee, and given your name and address - that's how it used to be done, if I recollect. Still, perhaps, I can manage it for a trifling fee.'

'O, thank you! I would rather do it this way, as I should like it kept private.'

'Lover not to know, eh?'

'No - husband.'

'Aha! Very well. I'll get 'ee a touch of the corpse.'

'Where is it now?' she said, shuddering.

'It? - *he*, you mean; he's living yet. Just inside that little small winder up there in the glum.' He signified the jail on the cliff above.

She thought of her husband and her friends. 'Yes, of course,' she said; 'and how am I to proceed?'

He took her to the door. 'Now, do you be waiting at the little wicket in the wall, that you'll find up there in the lane, not later than one o'clock. I will open it from the inside, as I shan't come home to dinner till he's cut down. Good-night. Be punctual; and if you don't want anybody to know 'ee, wear a veil. Ah - once I had such a daughter as you!'

She went away, and climbed the path above, to assure herself that she would be able to find the wicket next day. Its outline was soon visible to her – a narrow opening in the outer wall of the prison precincts. The steep was so great that, having reached the wicket, she stopped a moment to breathe; and, looking back upon the water-side cot, saw the hangman again ascending his outdoor staircase. He entered the loft or chamber to which it led, and in a few minutes extinguished his light.

The town clock struck ten, and she returned to the White Hart as she had come.

A RENCOUNTER

IX

It was one o'clock on Saturday. Gertrude Lodge, having been admitted to the jail as above described, was sitting in a waiting-room within the second gate, which stood under a classic archway of ashlar, then comparatively modern, and bearing the inscription, 'COVNTY JAIL 1793'. This had been the façade she saw from the heath the day before. Near at hand was a passage to the roof on which the gallows stood.

The town was thronged, and the market suspended; but Gertrude had seen scarcely a soul. Having kept her room till the hour of the appointment, she had proceeded to the spot by a way which avoided the open space below the cliff where the spectators had gathered; but she could, even now, hear the multitudinous babble of their voices, out of which rose at intervals the hoarse croak of a single voice uttering the words, 'Last dying speech and confession!' There had been no reprieve, and the execution was over; but the crowd still waited to see the body taken down.

Soon the persistent woman heard a trampling overhead, then a hand beckoned to her, and, following directions, she went out and crossed the inner paved court beyond the gatehouse, her knees trembling so that she could scarcely walk. One of her arms was out of its sleeve, and only covered by her shawl.

On the spot at which she had now arrived were two trestles, and before she could think of their purpose she heard heavy feet descending stairs somewhere at her back. Turn her head she would not, or could not, and, rigid in this position, she was conscious of a rough coffin passing her shoulder, borne by four men. It was open, and in it lay the body of a young man, wearing the smockfrock of a rustic, and fustian breeches. The corpse had been thrown into the coffin so hastily that the skirt of the smockfrock was hanging over. The burden was temporarily deposited on the trestles.

By this time the young woman's state was such that a grey mist seemed to float before her eyes, on account of which, and the veil she wore, she could scarcely discern anything: it was as though she had nearly died, but was held up by a sort of galvanism.

'Now!' said a voice close at hand, and she was just conscious that the word had been addressed to her.

By a last strenuous effort she advanced, at the same time hearing persons approaching behind her. She bared her poor curst arm; and Davies, uncovering the face of the corpse, took Gertrude's hand, and held it so that her arm lay across the dead man's neck, upon a line the colour of an unripe blackberry, which surrounded it.

Gertrude shrieked: 'the turn o' the blood', predicted by the conjuror, had taken place. But at that moment a second shriek rent the air of the enclosure: it was not Gertrude's, and its effect upon her was to make her start round.

Immediately behind her stood Rhoda Brook, her face drawn, and her eyes red with weeping. Behind Rhoda stood Gertrude's own husband; his countenance lined, his eyes dim, but without a tear.

'D__n you! what are you doing here?' he said hoarsely.

'Hussy – to come between us and our child now!' cried

Rhoda. 'This is the meaning of what Satan showed me in the vision! You are like her at last!' And clutching the bare arm of the younger woman, she pulled her unresistingly back against the wall. Immediately Brook had loosened her hold the fragile young Gertrude slid down against the feet of her husband. When he lifted her up she was unconscious.

The mere sight of the twain had been long enough to suggest to her that the dead young man was Rhoda's son. At that time the relatives of an executed convict had the privilege of claiming the body for burial, if they chose to do so; and it was for this purpose that Lodge was awaiting the inquest with Rhoda. He had been summoned by her as soon as the young man was taken in the crime, and at different times since; and he had attended in court during the trial. This was the 'holiday' he had been indulging in of late. The two wretched parents had wished to avoid exposure; and hence had come themselves for the body, a waggon and sheet for its conveyance and covering being in waiting outside.

Gertrude's case was so serious that it was deemed advisable to call to her the surgeon who was at hand. She was taken out of the jail into the town; but she never reached home alive. Her delicate vitality, sapped perhaps by the paralysed arm, collapsed under the double shock that followed the severe strain, physical and mental, to which she had subjected herself during the previous twenty-four hours. Her blood had been 'turned' indeed – too far. Her death took place in the town three days after.

Her husband was never seen in Casterbridge again; once only in the old market-place at Anglebury, which he had so much frequented, and very seldom in public anywhere. Burdened at first with moodiness and remorse, he eventually changed for the better, and appeared as a chastened and thoughtful man. Soon after attending the funeral of his poor young wife he took steps towards giving up the farms in Holmstoke and the adjoining parish, and, having sold every head of his stock, he went away to Port-Bredy, at the other end of the county, living there in solitary lodgings till his death two years later of a painless decline. It was then found that he had bequeathed the whole of his not inconsiderable property to a reformatory for boys, subject to the payment of a small annuity to Rhoda Brook, if she could be found to claim it.

For some time she could not be found; but eventually she reappeared in her old parish, – absolutely refusing, however, to have anything to do with the provision made for her. Her monotonous milking at the dairy was resumed, and followed for many long years, till her form became bent, and her once abundant dark hair white and worn away at the forehead – perhaps by long pressure against the cows. Here, sometimes, those who knew her experiences would stand and observe her, and wonder what sombre thoughts were beating inside that impassive, wrinkled brow, to the rhythm of the alternating milk-streams.

THE SON'S VETO

TO the eyes of a man viewing it from behind, the nut-brown hair was a wonder and a mystery. Under the black beaver hat surmounted by its tuft of black feathers, the long locks, braided and twisted and coiled like the rushes of a basket, composed a rare, if somewhat barbaric, example of ingenious art. One could understand such weavings and coilings being wrought to last intact for a year, or even a calendar month; but that they should be all demolished regularly at bedtime, after a single day of permanence, seemed a reckless waste of successful fabrication.

And she had done it all herself, poor thing. She had no maid, and it was almost the only accomplishment she could boast of. Hence the unstinted pains.

She was a young invalid lady – not so very much of an invalid – sitting in a wheeled chair, which had been pulled up in the front part of a green enclosure, close to a bandstand where a concert was going on, during a warm June afternoon. It had place in one of the minor parks or private gardens that are to be found in the suburbs of London, and was the effort of a local association to raise money for some charity. There are worlds within worlds in the great city, and though nobody outside the immediate district had ever heard of the charity, or the band, or the garden, the enclosure was filled with an interested audience sufficiently informed on all these.

As the strains proceeded many of the listeners observed the chaired lady, whose back hair, by reason of her prominent position, so challenged inspection. Her face was not easily discernible, but the aforesaid cunning tress-weavings, the white ear and poll, and the curve of a cheek which was

neither flaccid nor sallow, were signals that led to the expec-
tation of good beauty in front. Such expectations are not
infrequently disappointed as soon as the disclosure comes;
and in the present case, when the lady, by a turn of the
head, at length revealed herself, she was not so handsome as
the people behind her had supposed, and even hoped – they
did not know why.

For one thing (alas! the commonness of this complaint),
she was less young than they had fancied her to be. Yet
attractive her face unquestionably was, and not at all sickly.
The revelation of its details came each time she turned to
talk to a boy of twelve or thirteen who stood beside her, and
the shape of whose hat and jacket implied that he belonged
to a well-known public school. The immediate bystanders
could hear that he called her 'Mother'.

When the end of the recital was reached, and the
audience withdrew, many chose to find their way out by
passing at her elbow. Almost all turned their heads to take a
full and near look at the interesting woman, who remained
stationary in the chair till the way should be clear enough for
her to be wheeled out without obstruction. As if she
expected their glances, and did not mind gratifying their
curiosity, she met the eyes of several of her observers by
lifting her own, showing these to be soft, brown, and affectionate orbs, a little plaintive in their regard.

She was conducted out of the gardens, and passed along
the pavement till she disappeared from view, the schoolboy
walking beside her. To inquiries made by some persons who
watched her away, the answer came that she was the second
wife of the incumbent of a neighbouring parish, and that
she was lame. She was generally believed to be a woman
with a story – an innocent one, but a story of some sort or
other.

In conversing with her on their way home the boy who
walked at her elbow said that he hoped his father had not
missed them.

'He have been so comfortable these last few hours that I am sure he cannot have missed us,' she replied.

'*Has*, dear mother – not *have*!' exclaimed the public-schoolboy, with an impatient fastidiousness that was almost harsh. 'Surely you know that by this time!'

His mother hastily adopted the correction, and did not resent his making it, or retaliate, as she might well have done, by bidding him to wipe that crumby mouth of his, whose condition had been caused by surreptitious attempts to eat a piece of cake without taking it out of the pocket wherein it lay concealed. After this the pretty woman and the boy went onward in silence.

That question of grammar bore upon her history, and she fell into reverie, of a somewhat sad kind to all appearance. It might have been assumed that she was wondering if she had done wisely in shaping her life as she had shaped it, to bring out such a result as this.

In a remote nook in North Wessex, forty miles from London, near the thriving county-town of Aldbrickham, there stood a pretty village with its church and parsonage, which she knew well enough, but her son had never seen. It was her native village, Gaymead, and the first event bearing upon her present situation had occurred at that place when she was only a girl of nineteen.

How well she remembered it, that first act in her little tragi-comedy, the death of her reverend husband's first wife. It happened on a spring evening, and she who now and for many years had filled that first wife's place was then parlour-maid in the parson's house.

When everything had been done that could be done, and the death was announced, she had gone out in the dusk to visit her parents, who were living in the same village, to tell them the sad news. As she opened the white swing-gate and looked towards the trees which rose westward, shutting out the pale light of the evening sky, she discerned, without much surprise, the figure of a man standing in the hedge, though she roguishly exclaimed as a matter of form, 'O, Sam, how you frightened me!'

He was a young gardener of her acquaintance. She told him the particulars of the late event, and they stood silent, these two young people, in that elevated, calmly philosophic mind which is engendered when a tragedy has happened close at hand, and has not happened to the philosophers themselves. But it had its bearing upon their relations.

'And will you stay on now at the Vicarage, just the same?' asked he.

She had hardly thought of that. 'O yes – I suppose!' she said. 'Everything will be just as usual, I imagine?'

He walked beside her towards her mother's. Presently his arm stole round her waist. She gently removed it; but he placed it there again, and she yielded the point. 'You see, dear Sophy, you don't know that you'll stay on; you may want a home; and I shall be ready to offer one some day, though I may not be ready just yet.'

'Why, Sam, how can you be so fast! I've never even said I liked 'ee; and it is all your own doing, coming after me!'

'Still, it is nonsense to say I am not to have a try at you like the rest.' He stooped to kiss her a farewell, for they had reached her mother's door.

'No, Sam; you sha'n't!' she cried, putting her hand over his mouth. 'You ought to be more serious on such a night as this.' And she bade him adieu without allowing him to kiss her or to come indoors.

The vicar just left a widower was at this time a man about forty years of age, of good family, and childless. He had led a secluded existence in this college living, partly because there were no resident landowners; and his loss now intensified his habit of withdrawal from outward observation. He was seen still less than heretofore, kept himself still less in time with the rhythm and racket of the movements called progress in the world without. For many months after his wife's decease the economy of his house-

hold remained as before; the cook, the housemaid, the parlour-maid, and the man out-of-doors performed their duties
or left them undone, just as Nature prompted them – the
vicar knew not which. It was then represented to him that
his servants seemed to have nothing to do in his small family
of one. He was struck with the truth of this representation,
and decided to cut down his establishment. But he was fore-
stalled by Sophy, the parlour-maid, who said one evening
that she wished to leave him.

'And why?' said the parson.

'Sam Hobson has asked me to marry him, sir.'

'Well – do you want to marry?'

'Not much. But it would be a home for me. And we have
heard that one of us will have to leave.'

A day or two after she said: 'I don't want to leave just yet,
sir, if you don't wish it. Sam and I have quarrelled.'

He looked up at her. He had hardly ever observed her
before, though he had been frequently conscious of her soft
presence in the room. What a kitten-like, flexuous, tender
creature she was! She was the only one of the servants with
whom he came into immediate and continuous relation.
What should he do if Sophy were gone?

Sophy did not go, but one of the others did, and things
went on quietly again.

When Mr Twycott, the vicar, was ill, Sophy brought up
his meals to him, and she had no sooner left the room one
day than he heard a noise on the stairs. She had slipped
down with the tray, and so twisted her foot that she could
not stand. The village surgeon was called in; the vicar got
better, but Sophy was incapacitated for a long time; and she
was informed that she must never again walk much or
engage in any occupation which required her to stand long
on her feet. As soon as she was comparatively well she spoke
to him alone. Since she was forbidden to walk and bustle
about, and, indeed, could not do so, it became her duty to
leave. She could very well work at something sitting down,

and she had an aunt a seamstress.

The parson had been very greatly moved by what she had suffered on his account, and he exclaimed, 'No, Sophy; lame or not lame, I cannot let you go. You must never leave me again!'

He came close to her, and, though she could never exactly tell how it happened, she became conscious of his lips upon her cheek. He then asked her to marry him. Sophy did not exactly love him, but she had a respect for him which almost amounted to veneration. Even if she had wished to get away from him she hardly dared refuse a personage so reverend and august in her eyes, and she assented forthwith to be his wife.

Thus it happened that one fine morning, when the doors of the church were naturally open for ventilation, and the singing birds fluttered in and alighted on the tie-beams of the roof, there was a marriage-service at the communion-rails, which hardly a soul knew of. The parson and a neighbouring curate had entered at one door, and Sophy at another, followed by two necessary persons, whereupon in a short time there emerged a newly-made husband and wife.

Mr Twycott knew perfectly well that he had committed social suicide by this step, despite Sophy's spotless character, and he had taken his measures accordingly. An exchange of livings had been arranged with an acquaintance who was incumbent of a church in the south of London, and as soon as possible the couple removed thither, abandoning their pretty home, with trees and shrubs and glebe, for a narrow, dusty house in a long, straight street, and their fine peal of bells for the wretchedest one-tongued clangour that ever tortured mortal ears. It was all on her account. They were, however, away from every one who had known her former position; and also under less observation from without than they would have had to put up with in any country parish.

Sophy the woman was as charming a partner as a man could possess, though Sophy the lady had her deficiencies. She showed a natural aptitude for little domestic refinements, so far as related to things and manners; but in what is called culture she was less intuitive. She had now been married more than fourteen years, and her husband had taken much trouble with her education; but she still held confused ideas on the use of 'was' and 'were', which did not beget a respect for her among the few acquaintances she made. Her great grief in this relation was that her only child, on whose education no expense had been and would be spared, was now old enough to perceive these deficiencies in his mother, and not only to see them but to feel irritated at their existence.

Thus she lived on in the city, and wasted hours in braiding her beautiful hair, till her once apple cheeks waned to pink of the very faintest. Her foot had never regained its natural strength after the accident, and she was mostly obliged to avoid walking altogether. Her husband had grown to like London for its freedom and its domestic privacy; but he was twenty years his Sophy's senior, and had latterly been seized with a serious illness. On this day, however, he had seemed to be well enough to justify her accompanying her son Randolph to the concert.

II

The next time we get a glimpse of her is when she appears in the mournful attire of a widow.

Mr Twycott had never rallied, and now lay in a well-packed cemetery to the south of the great city, where, if all the dead it contained had stood erect and alive, not one would have known him or recognized his name. The boy had dutifully followed him to the grave, and was now again at school.

Throughout these changes Sophy had been treated like the child she was in nature though not in years. She was left with no control over anything that had been her husband's beyond her modest personal income. In his anxiety lest her inexperience should be over-reached he had safeguarded with trustees all he possibly could. The completion of the boy's course at the public school, to be followed in due time by Oxford and ordination, had been all previsioned and arranged, and she really had nothing to occupy her in the world but to eat and drink, and make a business of indolence, and go on weaving and coiling the nut-brown hair, merely keeping a home open for the son whenever he came to her during vacations.

Foreseeing his probable decease long years before her, her husband in his lifetime had purchased for her use a semi-detached villa in the same long, straight road whereon the church and parsonage faced, which was to be hers as long as she chose to live in it. Here she now resided, looking out upon the fragment of lawn in front, and through the railings at the ever-flowing traffic; or, bending forward over the window-sill on the first floor, stretching her eyes far up and down the vista of sooty trees, hazy air, and drab house-façades, along which echoed the noises common to a suburban main thoroughfare.

Somehow, her boy, with his aristocratic school-knowledge, his grammars, and his aversions, was losing those wide infantine sympathies, extending as far as to the sun and moon themselves, with which he, like other children, had been born, and which his mother, a child of nature herself, had loved in him; he was reducing their compass to a population of a few thousand wealthy and titled people, the mere veneer of a thousand million or so of others who did not interest him at all. He drifted further and further away from her. Sophy's *milieu* being a suburb of minor tradesmen and under-clerks, and her almost only companions the two servants of her own house, it was not surprising that after her husband's death she soon lost the little artificial tastes she had acquired from him, and became – in her son's eyes – a mother whose mistakes and origin it was his painful lot as a gentleman to blush for. As yet he was far from being man enough – if he ever would be – to rate these sins of hers at their true infinitesimal value beside the yearning fondness that welled up and remained penned in her heart till it should be more fully accepted by him, or by some other person or thing. If he had lived at home with her he would have had all of it; but he seemed to require so very little in present circumstances, and it remained stored.

Her life became insupportably dreary; she could not take walks, and had no interest in going for drives, or, indeed, in travelling anywhere. Nearly two years passed without an event, and still she looked on that suburban road, thinking of the village in which she had been born, and whither she would have gone back – O how gladly! – even to work in the fields.

Taking no exercise she often could not sleep, and would rise in the night or early morning to look out upon the then vacant thoroughfare, where the lamps stood like sentinels waiting for some procession to go by. An approximation to such a procession was indeed made early every morning about one o'clock, when the country vehicles passed up with loads of vegetables for Covent Garden market. She often saw them creeping along at this silent and dusky hour – waggon after waggon, bearing green bastions of cabbages nodding to their fall, yet never falling, walls of baskets enclosing masses of beans and peas, pyramids of snow-white turnips, swaying howdahs of mixed produce – creeping along behind aged night-horses, who seemed ever patiently wondering between their hollow coughs why they had always to work at that still hour when all other sentient creatures were privileged to rest. Wrapped in a cloak, it was soothing to watch and sympathize with them when depression and nervousness hindered sleep, and to see how the

fresh green-stuff brightened to life as it came opposite the
lamp, and how the sweating animals steamed and shone
with their miles of travel.

They had an interest, almost a charm, for Sophy, these
semirural people and vehicles moving in an urban atmosphere, leading a life quite distinct from that of the daytime
toilers on the same road. One morning a man who accompanied a waggon-load of potatoes gazed rather hard at the
house-fronts as he passed, and with a curious emotion she
thought his form was familiar to her. She looked out for him
again. His being an old-fashioned conveyance, with a
yellow front, it was easily recognizable, and on the third
night after she saw it a second time. The man alongside was,
as she had fancied, Sam Hobson, formerly gardener at Gaymead, who would at one time have married her.

She had occasionally thought of him, and wondered if life
in a cottage with him would not have been a happier lot than
the life she had accepted. She had not thought of him
passionately, but her now dismal situation lent an interest to
his resurrection – a tender interest which it is impossible to
exaggerate. She went back to bed, and began thinking.
When did these market-gardeners, who travelled up to
town so regularly at one or two in the morning, come back?
She dimly recollected seeing their empty waggons, hardly
noticeable amid the ordinary day-traffic, passing down at
some hour before noon.

It was only April, but that morning, after breakfast, she
had the window opened, and sat looking out, the feeble sun
shining full upon her. She affected to sew, but her eyes never
left the street. Between ten and eleven the desired waggon,
now unladen, reappeared on its return journey. But Sam was
not looking round him then, and drove on in a reverie.

'Sam!' cried she.

Turning with a start, his face lighted up. He called to him
a little boy to hold the horse, alighted, and came and stood
under the window.

'I can't come down easily, Sam, or I would!' she said. 'Did you know I lived here?'

'Well, Mrs Twycott, I knew you lived along here somewhere. I have often looked out for 'ee.'

He briefly explained his own presence on the scene. He had long since given up his gardening in the village near Aldbrickham, and was now manager at a market-gardener's on the south side of London, it being part of his duty to go up to Covent Garden with waggon-loads of produce two or three times a week. In answer to her curious inquiry, he admitted that he had come to this particular district because he had seen in the Aldbrickham paper, a year or two before, the announcement of the death in South London of the aforetime vicar of Gaymead, which had revived an interest in her dwelling-place that he could not extinguish, leading him to hover about the locality till his present post had been secured.

They spoke of their native village in dear old North Wessex, the spots in which they had played together as children. She tried to feel that she was a dignified personage now, that she must not be too confidential with Sam. But she could not keep it up, and the tears hanging in her eyes were indicated in her voice.

'You are not happy, Mrs Twycott, I'm afraid?' he said.

'O, of course not! I lost my husband only the year before last.'

'Ah! I meant in another way. You'd like to be home again?'

'This is my home – for life. The house belongs to me. But I understand' – She let it out then. 'Yes, Sam, I long for home – *our* home! I *should* like to be there, and never leave it, and die there.' But she remembered herself. 'That's only a momentary feeling. I have a son, you know, a dear boy. He's at school now.'

'Somewhere handy, I suppose? I see there's lots on 'em along this road.'

'O no! Not in one of these wretched holes! At a public
school – one of the most distinguished in England.'

'Chok' it all! of course! I forget, ma'am, that you've been
a lady for so many years.

'No, I am not a lady,' she said sadly. 'I never shall be.
But he's a gentleman, and that – makes it – O how difficult
for me!'

III

The acquaintance thus oddly reopened proceeded apace.
She often looked out to get a few words with him, by night
or by day. Her sorrow was that she could not accompany
her one old friend on foot a little way, and talk more freely
than she could do while he paused before the house. One
night, at the beginning of June, when she was again on the
watch after an absence of some days from the window, he
entered the gate and said softly, 'Now, wouldn't some air
do you good? I've only half a load this morning. Why not
ride up to Covent Garden with me? There's a nice seat on
the cabbages, where I've spread a sack. You can be home
again in a cab before anybody is up.'

She refused at first, and then, trembling with excitement,
hastily finished her dressing, and wrapped herself up in
cloak and veil, afterwards sidling downstairs by the aid of
the handrail, in a way she could adopt on an emergency.
When she had opened the door she found Sam on the step,
and he lifted her bodily on his strong arm across the little
forecourt into his vehicle. Not a soul was visible or audible
in the infinite length of the straight, flat highway, with its
ever-waiting lamps converging to points in each direction.
The air was fresh as country air at this hour, and the stars
shone, except to the north-eastward, where there was a
whitish light – the dawn. Sam carefully placed her in the
seat, and drove on.

They talked as they had talked in old days, Sam pulling himself up now and then, when he thought himself too familiar. More than once she said with misgiving that she wondered if she ought to have indulged in the freak. 'But I am so lonely in my house,' she added, 'and this makes me so happy!'

'You must come again, dear Mrs Twycott. There is no time o' day for taking the air like this.'

It grew lighter and lighter. The sparrows became busy in the streets, and the city waxed denser around them. When they approached the river it was day, and on the bridge they beheld the full blaze of morning sunlight in the direction of St Paul's, the river glistening towards it, and not a craft stirring.

Near Covent Garden he put her into a cab, and they parted, looking into each other's faces like the very old friends they were. She reached home without adventure, limped to the door, and let herself in with her latch-key unseen.

The air and Sam's presence had revived her: her cheeks were quite pink – almost beautiful. She had something to live for in addition to her son. A woman of pure instincts, she knew there had been nothing really wrong in the journey, but supposed it conventionally to be very wrong indeed.

Soon, however, she gave way to the temptation of going with him again, and on this occasion their conversation was distinctly tender, and Sam said he never should forget her, notwithstanding that she had served him rather badly at one time. After much hesitation he told her of a plan it was in his power to carry out, and one he should like to take in hand, since he did not care for London work: it was to set up as a master greengrocer down at Aldbrickham, the county-town of their native place. He knew of an opening – a shop kept by aged people who wished to retire.

'And why don't you do it, then, Sam?' she asked with a slight heartsinking.

'Because I'm not sure if – you'd join me. I know you wouldn't – couldn't! Such a lady as ye've been so long, you couldn't be a wife to a man like me.'

'I hardly suppose I could!' she assented, also frightened at the idea.

'If you could,' he said eagerly, 'you'd on'y have to sit in the back parlour and look through the glass partition when I was away sometimes – just to keep an eye on things. The lameness wouldn't hinder that . . . I'd keep you as genteel as ever I could, dear Sophy – if I might think of it!' he pleaded.

'Sam, I'll be frank,' she said, putting her hand on his. 'If it were only myself I would do it, and gladly, though everything I possess would be lost to me by marrying again.'

'I don't mind that! It's more independent.'

'That's good of you, dear, dear Sam. But there's something else. I have a son . . . I almost fancy when I am miserable sometimes that he is not really mine, but one I hold in trust for my late husband. He seems to belong so little to me personally, so entirely to his dead father. He is so much educated and I so little that I do not feel dignified enough to be his mother . . . Well, he would have to be told.'

'Yes. Unquestionably.' Sam saw her thought and her fear. 'Still, you can do as you like, Sophy – Mrs Twycott,' he added. 'It is not you who are the child, but he.'

'Ah, you don't know! Sam, if I could, I would marry you, some day. But you must wait a while, and let me think.'

It was enough for him, and he was blithe at their parting. Not so she. To tell Randolph seemed impossible. She could wait till he had gone up to Oxford, when what she did would affect his life but little. But would he ever tolerate the idea? And if not, could she defy him?

She had not told him a word when the yearly cricket-match came on at Lord's between the public schools, though Sam had already gone back to Aldbrickham. Mrs Twycott felt stronger than usual: she went to the match with

Randolph, and was able to leave her chair and walk about occasionally. The bright idea occurred to her that she could casually broach the subject while moving round among the spectators, when the boy's spirits were high with interest in the game, and he would weigh domestic matters as feathers in the scale beside the day's victory. They promenaded under the lurid July sun, this pair, so wide apart, yet so near, and Sophy saw the large proportion of boys like her own, in their broad white collars and dwarf hats, and all around the rows of great coaches under which was jumbled the *débris* of luxurious luncheons; bones, pie-crusts, champagne-bottles, glasses, plates, napkins, and the family silver; while on the coaches sat the proud fathers and mothers; but never a poor mother like her. If Randolph had not appertained to these, had not centred all his interests in them, had not cared exclusively for the class they belonged to, how happy would things have been! A great huzza at some small performance with the bat burst from the multitude of relatives, and Randolph jumped wildly into the air to see what had happened. Sophy fetched up the sentence that had been already shaped; but she could not get it out. The occasion was, perhaps, an inopportune one. The contrast between her story and the display of fashion to which Randolph had grown to regard himself as akin would be fatal. She awaited a better time.

It was on an evening when they were alone in their plain suburban residence, where life was not blue but brown, that she ultimately broke silence, qualifying her announcement of a probable second marriage by assuring him that it would not take place for a long time to come, when he would be living quite independently of her.

The boy thought the idea a very reasonable one, and asked if she had chosen anybody? She hesitated; and he seemed to have a misgiving. He hoped his stepfather would be a gentleman? he said.

'Not what you call a gentleman,' she answered timidly.

'He'll be much as I was before I knew your father;' and by degrees she acquainted him with the whole. The youth's face remained fixed for a moment; then he flushed, leant on the table, and burst into passionate tears.

His mother went up to him, kissed all of his face that she could get at, and patted his back as if he were still the baby he once had been, crying herself the while. When he had somewhat recovered from his paroxysm he went hastily to his own room and fastened the door.

Parleyings were attempted through the keyhole, outside which she waited and listened. It was long before he would reply, and when he did it was to say sternly at her from within: 'I am ashamed of you! It will ruin me! A miserable boor! a churl! a clown! It will degrade me in the eyes of all the gentlemen of England!'

'Say no more – perhaps I am wrong! I will struggle against it!' she cried miserably.

Before Randolph left her that summer a letter arrived from Sam to inform her that he had been unexpectedly fortunate in obtaining the shop. He was in possession; it was the largest in the town, combining fruit with vegetables, and he thought it would form a home worthy even of her some day. Might he not run up to town to see her?

She met him by stealth, and said he must still wait for her final answer. The autumn dragged on, and when Randolph was home at Christmas for the holidays she broached the matter again. But the young gentleman was inexorable.

It was dropped for months; renewed again; abandoned under his repugnance; again attempted; and thus the gentle creature reasoned and pleaded till four or five long years had passed. Then the faithful Sam revived his suit with some peremptoriness. Sophy's son, now an undergraduate, was down from Oxford one Easter, when she again opened the subject. As soon as he was ordained, she argued, he would have a home of his own, wherein she, with her bad grammar and her ignorance, would be an encumbrance to him. Better obliterate her as much as possible.

He showed a more manly anger now, but would not agree. She on her side was more persistent, and he had doubts whether she could be trusted in his absence. But by indignation and contempt for her taste he completely maintained his ascendancy; and finally taking her before a little cross and altar that he had erected in his bedroom for his private devotions, there bade her kneel, and swear that she would not wed Samuel Hobson without his consent. 'I owe this to my father!' he said.

The poor woman swore, thinking he would soften as soon as he was ordained and in full swing of clerical work. But he did not. His education had by this time sufficiently ousted his humanity to keep him quite firm; though his mother might have led an idyllic life with her faithful fruiterer and greengrocer, and nobody have been anything the worse in the world.

Her lameness became more confirmed as time went on, and she seldom or never left the house in the long southern thoroughfare, where she seemed to be pining her heart away. 'Why mayn't I say to Sam that I'll marry him? Why mayn't I?' she would murmur plaintively to herself when nobody was near.

Some four years after this date a middle-aged man was standing at the door of the largest fruiterer's shop in Aldbrickham. He was the proprietor, but to-day, instead of his usual business attire, he wore a neat suit of black; and his window was partly shuttered. From the railway-station a funeral procession was seen approaching: it passed his door and went out of the town towards the village of Gaymead. The man, whose eyes were wet, held his hat in his hand as the vehicle moved by; while from the mourning coach a young smooth-shaven priest in a high waistcoat looked black as a cloud at the shop-keeper standing there.

TONY KYTES, THE ARCH-DECEIVER

'I shall never forget Tony's face,' said the carrier. ' 'Twas a little, round, firm, tight face, with a seam here and there left by the smallpox, but not enough to hurt his looks in a woman's eye, though he'd had it badish when he was a boy. So very serious looking and unsmiling 'a was, that young man, that it really seemed as if he couldn't laugh at all without great pain to his conscience. He looked very hard at a small speck in your eye when talking to 'ee. And there was no more sign of a whisker or beard on Tony Kytes's face than on the palm of my hand. He used to sing ''The Tailor's Breeches'' with a religious manner, as if it were a hymn: –

' ''O the petticoats went off, and the breeches they went on!''

and all the rest of the scandalous stuff. He was quite the women's favourite, and in return for their likings he loved 'em in shoals.

'But in course of time Tony got fixed down to one in particular, Milly Richards, a nice, light, small, tender little thing; and it was soon said that they were engaged to be married. One Saturday he had been to market to do business for his father, and was driving home the waggon in the afternoon. When he reached the foot of the very hill we shall be going over in ten minutes who should he see waiting for him at the top but Unity Sallet, a handsome girl, one of the young women he'd been very tender toward before he'd got engaged to Milly.

'As soon as Tony came up to her she said, ''My dear Tony, will you give me a lift home?''

' ''That I will, darling,'' said Tony. ''You don't suppose I could refuse 'ee?''

'She smiled a smile, and up she hopped, and on drove Tony.

' "Tony," she says, in a sort of tender chide, "why did ye desert me for that other one? In what is she better than I? I should have made 'ee a finer wife, and a more loving one too. 'Tisn't girls that are so easily won at first that are the best. Think how long we've known each other – ever since we were children almost – now haven't we, Tony?"

' "Yes, that we have," says Tony, a-struck with the truth o't.

' "And you've never seen anything in me to complain of, have ye, Tony? Now tell the truth to me?"

' "I never have, upon my life," says Tony.

' "And – can you say I'm not pretty, Tony? Now look at me!"

'He let his eyes light upon her for a long while. "I really can't," says he. "In fact, I never knowed you was so pretty before!"

' "Prettier than she?"

'What Tony would have said to that nobody knows, for before he could speak, what should he see ahead, over the hedge past the turning, but a feather he knew well – the feather in Milly's hat – she to whom he had been thinking of putting the question as to giving out the banns that very week.

' "Unity," says he, as mild as he could, "here's Milly coming. Now I shall catch it mightily if she sees 'ee riding here with me; and if you get down she'll be turning the corner in a moment, and, seeing 'ee in the road, she'll know we've been coming on together. Now, dearest Unity, will ye, to avoid all unpleasantness, which I know ye can't bear any more than I, will ye lie down in the back part of the waggon, and let me cover you over with the tarpaulin till Milly has passed? It will all be done in a minute. Do! – and I'll think over what we've said; and perhaps I shall put a loving question to you after all, instead of Milly. 'Tisn't true that it is all settled between her and me."

'Well, Unity Sallet agreed, and lay down at the back end

of the waggon, and Tony covered her over, so that the waggon seemed to be empty but for the loose tarpaulin; and then he drove on to meet Milly.

‘ ‘‘My dear Tony!’’ cries Milly, looking up with a little pout at him as he came near. ‘‘How long you’ve been coming home! Just as if I didn’t live at Upper Longpuddle at all! And I’ve come to meet you as you asked me to do, and to ride back with you, and talk over our future home – since you asked me, and I promised. But I shouldn’t have come else, Mr Tony!’’

‘ ‘‘Ay, my dear, I did ask ye – to be sure I did, now I think of it – but I had quite forgot it. To ride back with me, did you say, dear Milly?’’

‘ ‘‘Well, of course! What can I do else? Surely you don’t want me to walk, now I’ve come all this way?’’

‘ ‘‘O no, no! I was thinking you might be going on to town to meet your mother. I saw her there – and she looked as if she might be expecting ’ee.’’

‘ ‘‘O no; she’s just home. She came across the fields, and so got back before you.’’

‘ ‘‘Ah! I didn’t know that,’’ says Tony. And there was no help for it but to take her up beside him.

‘They talked on very pleasantly, and looked at the trees, and beasts, and birds, and insects, and at the ploughmen at work in the fields, till presently who should they see looking out of the upper window of a house that stood beside the road they were following, but Hannah Jolliver, another young beauty of the place at that time, and the very first woman that Tony had fallen in love with – before Milly and before Unity, in fact – the one that he had almost arranged to marry instead of Milly. She was a much more dashing girl than Milly Richards, though he’d not thought much of her of late. The house Hannah was looking from was her aunts’.

‘ ‘‘My dear Milly – my coming wife, as I may call ’ee,’’ says Tony in his modest way, and not so loud that Unity could overhear, "I see a young woman alooking out of window, who I think may accost me. The fact is, Milly, she had a notion that I was wishing to marry her, and since she's discovered I've promised another, and a prettier than she, I'm rather afeard of her temper if she sees us together. Now, Milly, would you do me a favour – my coming wife, as I may say?"

' "Certainly, dearest Tony," says she.

' "Then would ye creep under the empty sacks just here in the front of the waggon, and hide there out of sight till we've passed the house? She hasn't seen us yet. You see, we ought to live in peace and good-will since 'tis almost Christmas, and 'twill prevent angry passions rising, which we always should do."

' "I don't mind, to oblige you, Tony," Milly said; and though she didn't care much about doing it, she crept under, and crouched down just behind the seat, Unity being snug at the other end. So they drove on till they got near the road-side cottage. Hannah had soon seen him coming, and waited at the window, looking down upon him. She tosses her head a little disdainful and smiled off-hand.

' "Well, aren't you going to be civil enough to ask me to ride home with you!" she says, seeing that he was for driving past with a nod and a smile.

' "Ah, to be sure! What was I thinking of?" said Tony, in a flutter. "But you seem as if you was staying at your aunt's?"

' "No, I am not," she said. "Don't you see I have my bonnet and jacket on? I have only called to see her on my way home. How can you be so stupid, Tony?"

' "In that case – ah – of course you must come along wi' me," says Tony, feeling a dim sort of sweat rising up inside his clothes. And he reined in the horse and waited till she'd come downstairs, and then helped her up beside him. He drove on again, his face as long as a face that was a round one by nature well could be.

'Hannah looked round sideways into his eyes. "This is nice, isn't it, Tony?" she says. "I like riding with you."

'Tony looked back into her eyes. "And I with you," he said after a while. In short, having considered her, he warmed up, and the more he looked at her the more he liked her, till he couldn't for the life of him think why he had ever said a word about marriage to Milly or Unity while Hannah Jolliver was in question. So they sat a little closer and closer, their feet upon the foot-board and their shoulders touching, and Tony thought over and over again how handsome Hannah was. He spoke tenderer and tenderer, and called her "dear Hannah" in a whisper at last.

' "You've settled it with Milly by this time, I suppose," said she.

' "N–no, not exactly."

' "What? How low you talk, Tony."

' "Yes – I've a kind of hoarseness. I said, not exactly."

' "I suppose you mean to?"

' "Well, as to that –" His eyes rested on her face, and hers on his. He wondered how he could have been such a fool as not to follow up Hannah. "My sweet Hannah!" he bursts out, taking her hand, not being really able to help it, and forgetting Milly and Unity, and all the world besides. "Settled it? I don't think I have!"

' "Hark!" says Hannah.

' "What?" says Tony, letting go her hand.

' "Surely I heard a sort of little screaming squeak under those sacks? Why, you've been carrying corn, and there's mice in this waggon, I declare!" She began to haul up the tails of her gown.

' "Oh no; 'tis the axle," said Tony in an assuring way. "It do go like that sometimes in dry weather."

' "Perhaps it was . . . Well, now, to be quite honest, dear Tony, do you like her better than me? Because – because, although I've held off so independent, I'll own at last that I do like 'ee Tony, to tell the truth; and I wouldn't say no if you asked me – you know what.''

'Tony was so won over by this pretty offering mood of a girl who had been quite the reverse (Hannah had a backward way with her at times, if you can mind) that he just glanced behind, and then whispered very soft, ''I haven't quite promised her, and I think I can get out of it, and ask you that question you speak of.''

' ''Throw over Milly? – all to marry me! How delightful!'' broke out Hannah, quite loud, clapping her hands.

'At this there was a real squeak – an angry, spiteful squeak, and afterward a long moan, as if something had broke its heart, and a movement of the empty sacks.

' ''Somethings's there!'' said Hannah, starting up.

' ''It's nothing, really,'' says Tony in a soothing voice, and praying inwardly for a way out of this. ''I wouldn't tell 'ee at first, because I wouldn't frighten 'ee. But, Hannah, I've really a couple of ferrets in a bag under there, for rabbiting, and they quarrel sometimes. I don't wish it knowed, as 'twould be called poaching. Oh, they can't get out, bless ye – you are quite safe! And – and – what a fine day it is, isn't it, Hannah, for this time of year? Be you going to market next Saturday? How is your aunt now?'' And so on, says Tony, to keep her from talking any more about love in Milly's hearing.

'But he found his work cut out for him, and wondering again how he should get out of this ticklish business, he looked about for a chance. Nearing home he saw his father in a field not far off, holding up his hand as if he wished to speak to Tony.

' ''Would you mind taking the reins a moment, Hannah,'' he said, much relieved, ''while I go and find out what father wants?''

'She consented, and away he hastened into the field, only too glad to get breathing time. He found that his father was looking at him with rather a stern eye.

' ''Come, come, Tony,'' says old Mr Kytes, as soon as

his son was alongside him, "this won't do, you know."

' "What?" says Tony.

' "Why, if you mean to marry Milly Richards, do it, and there's an end o't. But don't go driving about the country with Jolliver's daughter and making a scandal. I won't have such things done."

' "I only asked her – that is, she asked me, to ride home."

' "She? Why, now, if it had been Milly, 'twould have been quite proper; but you and Hannah Jolliver going about by yourselves –"

' "Milly's there too, father."

' "Milly? Where?"

' "Under the corn-sacks! Yes, the truth is, father, I've got rather into a nunny-watch, I'm afeard! Unity Sallet is there too – yes, at the other end, under the tarpaulin. All three are in that waggon, and what to do with 'em I know no more than the dead! The best plan is, as I'm thinking, to speak out loud and plain to one of 'em before the rest, and that will settle it; not but what 'twill cause 'em to kick up a bit of a miff, for certain. Now which would you marry, father, if you was in my place?"

' "Whichever of 'em did *not* ask to ride with thee."

' "That was Milly, I'm bound to say, as she only mounted by my invitation. But Milly –"

' "Then stick to Milly, she's the best ... But look at that!"

'His father pointed toward the waggon. "She can't hold that horse in. You shouldn't have left the reins in her hands. Run on and take the horse's head, or there'll be some accident to them maids!"

'Tony's horse, in fact, in spite of Hannah's tugging at the reins, had started on his way at a brisk walking pace, being very anxious to get back to the stable, for he had had a long day out. Without another word Tony rushed away from his father to overtake the horse.

'Now of all things that could have happened to wean him from Milly there was nothing so powerful as his father's recommending her. No; it could not be Milly, after all. Hannah must be the one, since he could not marry all three. This he thought while running after the waggon. But queer things were happening inside it.

'It was, of course, Milly who had screamed under the sack-bags, being obliged to let off her bitter rage and shame in that way at what Tony was saying and never daring to show, for very pride and dread o' being laughed at, that she was in hiding. She became more and more restless, and in twisting herself about, what did she see but another woman's foot and white stocking close to her head. It quite frightened her, not knowing that Unity Sallet was in the waggon likewise. But after the fright was over she determined to get to the bottom of all this, and she crept and crept along the bed of the waggon, under the tarpaulin, like a snake, when lo and behold she came face to face with Unity.

' "Well, if this isn't disgraceful!" says Milly in a raging whisper to Unity.

' " 'Tis," says Unity, "to see you hiding in a young man's waggon like this, and no great character belonging to either of ye!"

' "Mind what you are saying!" replied Milly, getting louder. "I am engaged to be married to him, and haven't I a right to be here? What right have you, I should like to know? What has he been promising you? A pretty lot of nonsense, I expect! But what Tony says to other women is all mere wind, and no concern to me!"

' "Don't you be too sure!" says Unity. "He's going to have Hannah, and not you, nor me either; I could hear that."

'Now at these strange voices sounding from under the cloth Hannah was thunderstruck a'most into a swound; and it was just at this time that the horse moved on. Hannah tugged away wildly, not knowing what she was doing; and as the quarrel rose louder and louder Hannah got so horrified that she let go the reins altogether. The horse went on at his own pace, and coming to the corner where we turn round to drop down the hill to Lower Longpuddle he turned too quick, the off wheels went up the bank, the waggon rose sideways till it was quite on edge upon the near axles, and out rolled the three maidens into the road in a heap.

'When Tony came up, frightened and breathless, he was relieved enough to see that neither of his darlings was hurt, beyond a few scratches from the brambles of the hedge. But he was rather alarmed when he heard how they were going on at one another.

' "Don't ye quarrel, my dears – don't ye!" says he, taking off his hat out of respect to 'em. And then he would have kissed them all round, as fair and square as a man could, but they were in too much of a taking to let him, and screeched and sobbed till they was quite spent.

' "Now I'll speak out honest, because I ought to," says Tony, as soon as he could get heard. "And this is the truth," says he. "I've asked Hannah to be mine, and she is willing, and we are going to put up the banns next –"

'Tony had not noticed that Hannah's father was coming up behind, nor had he noticed that Hannah's face was beginning to bleed from the scratch of a bramble. Hannah had seen her father, and had run to him, crying worse than ever.

' "My daughter is *not* willing, sir!" says Mr Jolliver hot and strong. "Be you willing, Hannah? I ask ye to have spirit enough to refuse him, if yer virtue is left to 'ee and you run no risk?"

' "She's as sound as a bell for me, that I'll swear!" says Tony flaring up. "And so's the others, come to that, though you may think it an onusual thing in me!"

' "I have spirit, and I do refuse him!" says Hannah, partly because her father was there, and partly, too, in a tantrum because of the discovery, and the scratch on her face. "Little did I think when I was so soft with him just now that I was talking to such a false deceiver!"

' "What, you won't have me, Hannah?" says Tony, his jaw hanging down like a dead man'.

' "Never – I would sooner marry no – nobody at all!" she gasped out, though with her heart in her throat, for she would not have refused Tony if he had asked her quietly, and her father had not been there, and her face had not been scratched by the bramble. And having said that, away she walked upon her father's arm, thinking and hoping he would ask her again.

'Tony didn't know what to say next. Milly was sobbing her heart out; but as his father had strongly recommended her he couldn't feel inclined that way so he turned to Unity.

' "Well, will you, Unity dear, be mine?" he says.

' "Take her leavings? Not I!" says Unity. "I'd scorn it!" And away walks Unity Sallet likewise, though she looked back when she'd gone some way, to see if he was following her.

'So there at last were left Milly and Tony by themselves, she crying in watery streams, and Tony looking like a tree struck by lightning.

' "Well, Milly," he says at last, going up to her, "it do seem as if fate had ordained that it should be you and I, or nobody. And what must be must be, I suppose. Hey, Milly?"

' "If you like, Tony. You didn't really mean what you said to them?"

' "Not a word of it!" declares Tony, bringing down his fist upon his palm.

'And then he kissed her, and put the waggon to rights, and they mounted together; and their banns were put up the very next Sunday. I was not able to go to their wedding, but it was a rare party they had, by all account. Everybody in Longpuddle was there almost.'

ABSENT-MINDEDNESS IN A PARISH CHOIR

'IT happened on Sunday after Christmas – the last Sunday ever they played in Longpuddle church gallery, as it turned out, though they didn't know it then. As you may know, sir, the players formed a very good band – almost as good as the Mellstock parish players that were led by the Dewys; and that's saying a great deal. There was Nicholas Pudding-come, the leader, with the first fiddle; there was Timothy Thomas, the bass-viol man; John Biles, the tenor fiddler; Dan'l Hornhead, with the serpent; Robert Dowdle, with the clarionet; and Mr Nicks, with the oboe – all sound and powerful musicians, and strong-winded men – they that blowed. For that reason they were very much in demand Christmas week for little reels and dancing parties; for they could turn a jig or a hornpipe out of hand as well as ever they could turn out a psalm, and perhaps better, not to speak irreverent. In short, one half-hour they could be playing a Christmas carol in the squire's hall to the ladies and gentlemen, and drinking tay and coffee with 'em as modest as saints; and the next, at The Tinker's Arms, blazing away like wild horses with the "Dashing White Sergeant" to nine couple of dancers and more, and swallowing rum-and-cider hot as flame.

'Well, this Christmas they'd been out to one rattling randy after another every night, and had got next to no sleep at all. Then came the Sunday after Christmas their fatal day. 'Twas so mortal cold that year that they could hardly sit in the gallery; for though the congregation down in the body of the church had a stove to keep off the frost, the players in the gallery had nothing at all. So Nicholas said at morning service, when 'twas freezing an inch an hour, "Please the Lord I won't stand this numbing weather no longer: this afternoon we'll have something in our insides to make us warm, if it cost a king's ransom.''

'So he brought a gallon of hot brandy and beer, ready mixed, to church with him in the afternoon, and by keeping the jar well wrapped up in Timothy Thomas's bass-viol bag it kept drinkably warm till they wanted it, which was just a thimbleful in the Absolution, and another after the Creed, and the remainder at the beginning o' the sermon. When they'd had the last pull they felt quite comfortable and warm, and as the sermon went on – most unfortunately for 'em it was a long one that afternoon – they fell asleep, every man jack of 'em; and there they slept on as sound as rocks.

' "'Twas a very dark afternoon, and by the end of the sermon all you could see of the inside of the church were the pa'son's two candles alongside of him in the pulpit, and his spaking face behind 'em. The sermon being ended at last, the pa'son gie'd out the Evening Hymn. But no choir set about sounding up the tune, and the people began to turn their heads to learn the reason why, and then Levi Limpet, a boy who sat in the gallery, nudged Timothy and Nicholas, and said, "Begin! begin!''

' "Hey? what?'' says Nicholas, starting up; and the church being so dark and his head so muddled he thought he was at the party they had played at all the night before, and away he went, bow and fiddle, at "The Devil among the Tailors,'' the favourite jig of our neighbourhood at that time. The rest of the band, being in the same state of mind and nothing doubting, followed their leader with all their strength, according to custom. They poured out that there tune till the lower bass notes of "The Devil among the Tailors'' made the cobwebs in the roof shiver like ghosts; then Nicholas, seeing nobody moved, shouted out as he scraped (in his usual commanding way at dances when the folk didn't know the figures), "Top couples cross hands! And when I make the fiddle squeak at the end, every man kiss his pardner under the mistletoe!''

'The boy Levi was so frightened that he bolted down the gallery stairs and out homeward like lightning. The pa'son's hair fairly stood on end when he heard the evil tune raging through the church, and thinking the choir had gone crazy he held up his hand and said: "Stop, stop, stop! Stop, stop! What's this?" But they didn't hear'n for the noise of their own playing, and the more he called the louder they played.

'Then the folks came out of their pews, wondering down to the ground, and saying: "What do they mean by such wickedness! We shall be consumed like Sodom and Gomorrah!"

'Then the squire came out of his pew lined wi' green baize, where lots of lords and ladies visiting at the house were worshipping along with him, and went and stood in front of the gallery, and shook his fist in the musicians' faces saying, "What! In this reverent edifice! What!"

'And at last they heard'n through their playing, and stopped.

' "Never such an insulting, disgraceful thing – never!" says the squire, who couldn't rule his passion.

' "Never!" says the pa'son, who had come down and stood beside him.

' "Not if the Angels of Heaven," says the squire (he was a wickedish man, the squire was, though now for once he happened to be on the Lord's side) – "not if the Angels of Heaven come down," he says, "shall one of you villainous players ever sound a note in this church again; for the insult to me, and my family, and my visitors, and God Almighty, that you've a-perpetrated this afternoon!"

'Then the unfortunate church band came to their senses, and remembered where they were; and 'twas a sight to see Nicholas Puddingcome and Timothy Thomas and John Biles creep down the gallery stairs with their fiddles under their arms and, poor Dan'l Hornhead with his serpent, and Robert Dowdle with his clarionet, all looking as little as ninepins; and out they went.The pa'son might have forgi'ed 'em when he learned the truth o't, but the squire would not. That very week he sent for a barrel-organ that would play two-and-twenty new psalm-tunes, so exact and particular that, however sinful inclined you was, you could play nothing but psalm-tunes whatsomever. He had a really respectable man to turn the winch, as I said, and the old players played no more.'

THE MELANCHOLY HUSSAR OF THE
GERMAN LEGION

I

HERE stretch the downs; high and breezy and green, absolutely unchanged since those eventful days. A plough has never disturbed the turf, and the sod that was uppermost then is uppermost now. Here stood the camp; here are distinct traces of the banks thrown up for the horses of the cavalry, and spots where the midden-heaps lay are still to be observed. At night, when I walk across the lonely place, it is impossible to avoid hearing, amid the scourings of the wind over the grass-bents and thistles, the old trumpet and bugle calls, the rattle of the halters; to help seeing rows of spectral tents and the *impedimenta* of the soldiery. From within the canvases come guttural syllables of foreign tongues, and broken songs of the fatherland; for they were mainly regiments of the King's German Legion that slept round the tent-poles hereabout at that time.

It was nearly ninety years ago. The British uniform of the period, with its immense epaulettes, queer cocked-hat, breeches, gaiters, ponderous cartridge-box, buckled shoes, and what not, would look strange and barbarous now. Ideas have changed; invention has followed invention. Soldiers were monumental objects then. A divinity still hedged kings here and there; and war was considered a glorious thing.

Secluded old manor-houses and hamlets lie in the ravines and hollows among these hills, where a stranger had hardly ever been seen till the King chose to take the baths yearly at the sea-side watering-place a few miles to the south; as a consequence of which battalions descended in a cloud upon the open country around. Is it necessary to add that the echoes of many characteristic tales, dating from that picturesque time, still linger about here in more or less fragmentary form, to be caught by the attentive ear? Some of them I have repeated; most of them I have forgotten; one I have never repeated, and assuredly can never forget.

Phyllis told me the story with her own lips. She was then an old lady of seventy-five, and her auditor a lad of fifteen. She enjoined silence as to her share of the incident, till she should be 'dead, buried, and forgotten'. Her life was prolonged twelve years after the day of her narration, and she has now been dead nearly twenty. The oblivion which in her modesty and humility she courted for herself has only partially fallen on her, with the unfortunate result of inflicting an injustice upon her memory; since such fragments of her story as got abroad at the time, and have been kept alive ever since, are precisely those which are most unfavourable to her character.

It all began with the arrival of the York Hussars; one of the foreign regiments above alluded to. Before that day scarcely a soul had been seen near her father's house for weeks. When a noise like the brushing skirt of a visitor was heard on the doorstep, it proved to be a scudding leaf; when a carriage seemed to be nearing the door, it was her father grinding his sickle on the stone in the garden for his favourite relaxation of trimming the box-tree borders to the plots. A sound like luggage thrown down from the coach was a gun far away at sea; and what looked like a tall man by the gate at dusk was a yew bush cut into a quaint and attenuated shape. There is no such solitude in country places now as there was in those old days.

Yet all the while King George and his court were at his favourite sea-side resort, not more than five miles off.

The daughter's seclusion was great, but beyond the seclusion of the girl lay the seclusion of the father. If her social condition was twilight, his was darkness. Yet he enjoyed his darkness, while her twilight oppressed her. Dr Grove had been a professional man whose taste for lonely meditation over metaphysical questions had diminished his practice till it no longer paid him to keep it going; after which he had relinquished it and hired at a nominal rent the small, dilapidated, half farm half manor-house of this obscure inland nook, to make a sufficiency of an income which in a town would have been inadequate for their maintenance. He stayed in his garden the greater part of the day, growing more and more irritable with the lapse of time, and the increasing perception that he had wasted his life in the pursuit of illusions. He saw his friends less and less frequently. Phyllis became so shy that if she met a stranger anywhere in her short rambles she felt ashamed at his gaze, walked awkwardly, and blushed to her shoulders.

Yet Phyllis was discovered even here by an admirer, and her hand most unexpectedly asked in marriage.

The King, as aforesaid, was at the neighbouring town, where he had taken up his abode at Gloucester Lodge; and his presence in the town naturally brought many county people thither. Among these idlers – many of whom professed to have connections and interests with the Court – was one Humphrey Gould, a bachelor; a personage neither young nor old; neither good-looking nor positively plain. Too steady-going to be 'a buck' (as fast and unmarried men were then called), he was an approximately fashionable man of a mild type. This bachelor of thirty found his way to the village on the down: beheld Phyllis; made her father's acquaintance in order to make hers; and by some means or other she sufficiently inflamed his heart to lead him in that direction almost daily; till he became engaged to marry her.

As he was of an old local family, some of whose members were held in respect in the county, Phyllis, in bringing him to her feet, had accomplished what was considered a brilliant move for one in her constrained position. How she had done it was not quite known to Phyllis herself. In those days unequal marriages were regarded rather as a violation of the laws of nature than as a mere infringement of convention, the more modern view, and hence when Phyllis, of the watering-place *bourgeoisie*, was chosen by such a gentlemanly fellow, it was as if she were going to be taken to heaven, though perhaps the uninformed would have seen no great difference in the respective positions of the pair, the said Gould being as poor as a crow.

This pecuniary condition was his excuse – probably a true one – for postponing their union, and as the winter drew nearer, and the King departed for the season, Mr Humphrey Gould set out for Bath, promising to return to Phyllis in a few weeks. The winter arrived, the date of his promise passed, yet Gould postponed his coming, on the ground that he could not very easily leave his father in the city of their sojourn, the elder having no other relative near him. Phyllis, though lonely in the extreme, was content. The man who had asked her in marriage was a desirable husband for her in many ways; her father highly approved of his suit; but this neglect of her was awkward, if not painful, for Phyllis. Love him in the true sense of the word she assured me she never did, but she had a genuine regard for him; admired a certain methodical and dogged way in which he sometimes took his pleasure; valued his knowledge of what the Court was doing, had done, or was about to do; and she was not without a feeling of pride that he had chosen her when he might have exercised a more ambitious choice.

But he did not come; and the spring developed. His letters were regular though formal; and it is not to be wondered that the uncertainty of her position, linked with the fact that there was not much passion in her thoughts of Humphrey, bred an indescribable dreariness in the heart of Phyllis Grove. The spring was soon summer, and the summer brought the King; but still no Humphrey Gould. All this while the engagement by letter was maintained intact.

At this point of time a golden radiance flashed in upon the lives of people here, and charged all youthful thought with emotional interest. This radiance was the aforesaid York Hussars.

II

The present generation has probably but a very dim notion of the celebrated York Hussars of ninety years ago. They were one of the regiments of the King's German Legion, and (though they somewhat degenerated later on) their brilliant uniform, their splendid horses, and above all, their foreign air and mustachios (rare appendages then), drew crowds of admirers of both sexes wherever they went. These with other regiments had come to encamp on the downs and pastures, because of the presence of the King in the neighbouring town.

The spot was high and airy, and the view extensive, commanding Portland – the Isle of Slingers – in front, and reaching to St Aldhelm's Head eastward, and almost to the Start on the west.

Phyllis, though not precisely a girl of the village, was as interested as any of them in this military investment. Her father's home stood somewhat apart, and on the highest point of ground to which the lane ascended, so that it was almost level with the top of the church tower in the lower part of the parish. Immediately from the outside of the garden-wall the grass spread away to a great distance, and it was crossed by a path which came close to the wall. Ever since her childhood it had been Phyllis's pleasure to clamber up this fence and sit on the top – a feat not so difficult as it may seem, the walls in this district being built of rubble, without mortar, so that there were plenty of crevices for small toes.

She was sitting up here one day, listlessly surveying the pasture without, when her attention was arrested by a solitary figure walking along the path. It was one of the renowned German Hussars, and he moved onward with his eyes on the ground, and with the manner of one who wished to escape company. His head would probably have been bent like his eyes but for his stiff neck-gear. On nearer view she perceived that his face was marked with deep sadness. Without observing her, he advanced by the footpath till it brought him almost immediately under the wall.

Phyllis was much surprised to see a fine, tall soldier in such a mood as this. Her theory of the military, and of the York Hussars in particular (derived entirely from hearsay, for she had never talked to a soldier in her life), was that their hearts were as gay as their accoutrements.

At this moment the Hussar lifted his eyes and noticed her on her perch, the white muslin neckerchief which covered her shoulders and neck where left bare by her low gown, and her white raiment in general, showing conspicuously in the bright sunlight of this summer day. He blushed a little at the suddenness of the encounter, and without halting a moment from his pace passed on.

All that day the foreigner's face haunted Phyllis; its aspect was so striking, so handsome, and his eyes were so blue, and sad, and abstracted. It was perhaps only natural that on some following day at the same hour she should look over that wall again, and wait till he had passed a second time. On this occasion he was reading a letter, and at the sight of her his manner was that of one who had half expected or hoped to discover her. He almost stopped, smiled, and made a courteous salute. The end of the meeting was that they exchanged a few words. She asked him what he was reading, and he readily informed her that he was re-perusing letters from his mother in Germany; he did not get them often, he said, and was forced to read the old ones a great many times. This was all that passed at the present interview, but others of the same kind followed.

Phyllis used to say that his English, though not good, was quite intelligible to her, so that their acquaintance was never hindered by difficulties of speech. Whenever the subject became too delicate, subtle, or tender, for such words of English as were at his command, the eyes no doubt helped out the tongue, and – though this was later on – the lips helped out the eyes. In short this acquaintance, unguardedly made, and rash enough on her part, developed and ripened. Like Desdemona, she pitied him, and learnt his history.

His name was Matthäus Tina, and Saarbrück his native town, where his mother was still living. His age was twenty-two, and he had already risen to the grade of corporal, though he had not long been in the army. Phyllis used to assert that no such refined or well-educated young man could have been found in the ranks of the purely English regiments, some of these foreign soldiers having rather the graceful manner and presence of our native officers than of our rank and file.

She by degrees learnt from her foreign friend a circumstance about himself and his comrades which Phyllis would least have expected of the York Hussars. So far from being as gay as its uniform, the regiment was pervaded by a dreadful melancholy, a chronic home-sickness, which depressed many of the men to such an extent that they could hardly attend to their drill. The worst sufferers were the younger soldiers who had not been over here long. They hated England and English life; they took no interest whatever in King George and his island kingdom, and they only wished to be out of it and never to see it any more. Their bodies were here, but their hearts and minds were always far away in their dear fatherland, of which – brave men and stoical as they were in many ways – they would speak with tears in their eyes. One of the worst of the sufferers from this home-woe, as he called it in his own tongue, was Matthäus Tina, whose dreamy musing nature felt the gloom of exile still more intensely from the fact that he had left a lonely mother at home with nobody to cheer her.

Though Phyllis, touched by all this, and interested in his

history, did not disdain her soldier's acquaintance, she declined (according to her own account, at least) to permit the young man to overstep the line of mere friendship for a long while – as long, indeed, as she considered herself likely to become the possession of another; though it is probable that she had lost her heart to Matthäus before she was herself aware. The stone wall of necessity made anything like intimacy difficult; and he had never ventured to come, or to ask to come, inside the garden, so that all their conversation had been overtly conducted across this boundary.

III

But news reached the village from a friend of Phyllis's father concerning Mr Humphrey Gould, her remarkably cool and patient betrothed. This gentleman had been heard to say in Bath that he considered his overtures to Miss Phyllis Grove to have reached only the stage of a half-understanding; and in view of his enforced absence on his father's account, who was too great an invalid now to attend to his affairs, he thought it best that there should be no definite promise as yet on either side. He was not sure, indeed, that he might not cast his eyes elsewhere.

This account – though only a piece of hearsay, and as such entitled to no absolute credit – tallied so well with the infrequency of his letters and their lack of warmth, that Phyllis did not doubt its truth for one moment; and from that hour she felt herself free to bestow her heart as she should choose. Not so her father; he declared the whole story to be a fabrication. He had known Mr Gould's family from his boyhood; and if there was one proverb which expressed the matrimonial aspect of that family well, it was 'Love me little, love me long.' Humphrey was an honourable man, who would not think of treating his engagement so lightly. 'Do you wait in patience,' he said; 'all will be right in time.'

From these words Phyllis at first imagined that her father was in correspondence with Mr Gould; and her heart sank within her; for in spite of her original intentions she had been relieved to hear that her engagement had come to nothing. But she presently learnt that her father had heard no more of Humphrey Gould than she herself had done; while he would not write and address her affianced directly on the subject, lest it should be deemed an imputation on that bachelor's honour.

'You want an excuse for encouraging one or other of those foreign fellows to flatter you with his unmeaning attentions,' her father exclaimed, his mood having of late been a very unkind one towards her. 'I see more than I say. Don't you ever set foot outside that garden-fence without my permission. If you want to see that camp I'll take you myself some Sunday afternoon.'

Phyllis had not the smallest intention of disobeying him in her actions, but she assumed herself to be independent with respect to her feelings. She no longer checked her fancy for the Hussar, though she was far from regarding him as her lover in the serious sense in which an Englishman might have been regarded as such. The young foreign soldier was almost an ideal being to her, with none of the appurtenances of an ordinary house-dweller; one who had descended she knew not whence, and would disappear she knew not whither; the subject of a fascinating dream – no more.

They met continually now – mostly at dusk – during the brief interval between the going down of the sun and the minute at which the last trumpet-call summoned him to his tent. Perhaps her manner had become less restrained latterly; at any rate that of the Hussar was so; he had grown more tender every day, and at parting after these hurried interviews she reached down her hand from the top of the wall that he might press it. One evening he held it such a while that she exclaimed, 'The wall is white, and somebody in the field may see your shape against it!'

He lingered so long that night that it was with the greatest difficulty that he could run across the intervening stretch of ground and enter the camp in time. On the next occasion of his awaiting her she did not appear in her usual place at the usual hour. His disappointment was unspeakably keen; he remained staring blankly at the spot, like a man in a trance. The trumpets and tattoo sounded, and still he did not go.

She had been delayed purely by an accident. When she arrived she was anxious because of the lateness of the hour, having heard as well as he the sounds denoting the closing of the camp. She implored him to leave immediately.

'No,' he said gloomily. 'I shall not go in yet – the moment you come – I have thought of your coming all day.'

'But you may be disgraced at being after time?'

'I don't mind that. I should have disappeared from the world some time ago if it had not been for two persons – my beloved, here, and my mother in Saarbrück. I hate the army. I care more for a minute of your company than for all the promotion in the world.'

Thus he stayed and talked to her, and told her interesting details of his native place, and incidents of his childhood, till she was in a simmer of distress at his recklessness in remaining. It was only because she insisted on bidding him good-night and leaving the wall that he returned to his quarters.

The next time that she saw him he was without the stripes that had adorned his sleeve. He had been broken to the level of private for his lateness that night; and as Phyllis considered herself to be the cause of his disgrace her sorrow was great. But the position was now reversed; it was his turn to cheer her.

'Don't grieve, meine Liebliche!' he said. 'I have got a remedy for whatever comes. First, even supposing I regain my stripes, would your father allow you to marry a non-commissioned officer in the York Hussars?'

She flushed. This practical step had not been in her mind

in relation to such an unrealistic person as he was; and a moment's reflection was enough for it. 'My father would not – certainly would not,' she answered unflinchingly. 'It cannot be thought of! My dear friend, please do forget me: I fear I am ruining you and your prospects!'

'Not at all!' said he. 'You are giving this country of yours just sufficient interest to me to make me care to keep alive in it. If my dear land were here also, and my old parent, with you, I could be happy as I am, and would do my best as a soldier. But it is not so. And now listen. This is my plan. That you go with me to my own country, and be my wife there, and live there, with my mother and me. I am not a Hanoverian, as you know, though I entered the army as such; my country is by the Saar, and is at peace with France, and if I were once in it I should be free.'

'But how get there?' she asked. Phyllis had been rather amazed than shocked at his proposition. Her position in her father's house was growing irksome and painful in the extreme; his parental affection seemed to be quite dried up. She was not a native of the village, like all the joyous girls around her; and in some way Matthäus Tina had infected her with his own passionate longing for his country, and mother, and home.

'But how?' she repeated, finding that he did not answer. 'Will you buy your discharge?'

'Ah, no,' he said. 'That's impossible in these times. No; I came here against my will; why should I not escape? Now is the time, as we shall soon be striking camp, and I might see you no more. This is my scheme. I will ask you to meet me on the highway two miles off, on some calm night next week that may be appointed. There will be nothing unbecoming in it, or to cause you shame; you will not fly alone with me, for I will bring with me my devoted young friend Christoph, an Alsatian, who has lately joined the regiment, and who has agreed to assist in this enterprise. We shall have come from yonder harbour, where we shall have examined the boats, and found one suited to our purpose. Christoph has already a chart of the Channel, and we will then go to the harbour, and at midnight cut the boat from her moorings, and row away round the point out of sight; and by the next morning we are on the coast of France, near Cherbourg. The rest is easy, for I have saved money for the land journey, and can get a change of clothes. I will write to my mother, who will meet us on the way.'

He added details in reply to her inquiries, which left no doubt in Phyllis's mind of the feasibility of the undertaking. But its magnitude almost appalled her; and it is questionable if she would ever have gone further in the wild adventure if, on entering the house that night, her father had not accosted her in the most significant terms.

'How about the York Hussars?' he said.

'They are still at the camp; but they are soon going away, I believe.'

'It is useless for you to attempt to cloak your actions in that way. You have been meeting one of those fellows; you have been seen walking with him – foreign barbarians, not much better than the French themselves! I have made up my mind – don't speak a word till I have done, please! – I have made up my mind that you shall stay here no longer while they are on the spot. You shall go to your aunt's.'

It was useless for her to protest that she had never taken a walk with any soldier or man under the sun except himself. Her protestations were feeble, too, for though he was not literally correct in his assertion, he was virtually only half in error.

The house of her father's sister was a prison to Phyllis. She had quite recently undergone experience of its gloom; and when her father went on to direct her to pack what would be necessary for her to take, her heart died within her. In after years she never attempted to excuse her conduct during this week of agitation; but the result of her self-communing was that she decided to join in the scheme of her lover and his friend, and fly to the country which he had coloured with such lovely hues in her imagination. She always said that the one feature in his proposal which overcame her hesitation was the obvious purity and straightforwardness of his intentions. He showed himself to be so virtuous and kind; he treated her with a respect to which she had never before been accustomed; and she was braced to the obvious risks of the voyage by her confidence in him.

IV

It was on a soft, dark evening of the following week that they engaged in the adventure. Tina was to meet her at a point in the highway at which the lane to the village branched off. Christoph was to go ahead of them to the harbour where the boat lay, row it round the Nothe – or Look-out as it was called in those days – and pick them up on the other side of the promontory, which they were to reach by crossing the harbour-bridge on foot, and climbing over the Look-out hill.

As soon as her father had ascended to his room she left the house, and, bundle in hand, proceeded at a trot along the lane. At such an hour not a soul was afoot anywhere in the village, and she reached the junction of the lane with the highway unobserved. Here she took up her position in the obscurity formed by the angle of a fence, whence she could discern every one who approached along the turnpike road, without being herself seen.

She had not remained thus waiting for her lover longer than a minute – though from the tension of her nerves the lapse of even that short time was trying – when, instead of the expected footsteps, the stage-coach could be heard descending the hill. She knew that Tina would not show himself till the road was clear, and waited impatiently for the coach to pass. Nearing the corner where she was it slackened speed, and, instead of going by as usual, drew up within a few yards of her. A passenger alighted, and she heard his voice. It was Humphrey Gould's.

He had brought a friend with him, and luggage. The luggage was deposited on the grass, and the coach went on its route to the royal watering-place.

'I wonder where that young man is with the horse and trap?' said her former admirer to his companion. 'I hope we shan't have to wait here long. I told him half-past nine o'clock precisely.'

'Have you got her present safe?'

'Phyllis's? O, yes. It is in this trunk. I hope it will please her.'

'Of course it will. What woman would not be pleased with such a handsome peace-offering?'

'Well – she deserves it. I've treated her rather badly. But she has been in my mind these last two days much more than I should care to confess to everybody. Ah, well; I'll say no more about that. It cannot be that she is so bad as they make out. I am quite sure that a girl of her good wit would know better than to get entangled with any of those Hanoverian soldiers. I won't believe it of her, and there's an end on't.'

More words in the same strain were casually dropped as the two men waited; words which revealed to her, as by a sudden illumination, the enormity of her conduct. The conversation was at length cut off by the arrival of the man with the vehicle. The luggage was placed in it, and they mounted, and were driven on in the direction from which she had just come.

Phyllis was so conscience-stricken that she was at first inclined to follow them; but a moment's reflection led her to feel that it would only be bare justice to Matthäus to wait till he arrived, and explain candidly that she had changed her mind – difficult as the struggle would be when she stood face to face with him. She bitterly reproached herself for having believed reports which represented Humphrey Gould as false to his engagement, when, from what she now heard from his own lips, she gathered that he had been living full of trust in her. But she knew well enough who had won her love. Without him her life seemed a dreary prospect, yet the more she looked at his proposal the more she feared to accept it – so wild as it was, so vague, so venturesome. She had promised Humphrey Gould, and it was only his assumed faithlessness which had led her to treat that promise as nought. His solicitude in bringing her these gifts touched her; her promise must be kept, and esteem must take the place of love. She would preserve her self-respect. She would stay at home, and marry him, and suffer.

Phyllis had thus braced herself to an exceptional fortitude when, a few minutes later, the outline of Matthäus Tina appeared behind a field-gate, over which he lightly leapt as she stepped forward. There was no evading it, he pressed her to his breast.

'It is the first and last time!' she wildly thought as she stood encircled by his arms.

How Phyllis got through the terrible ordeal of that night she could never clearly recollect. She always attributed her success in carrying out her resolve to her lover's honour, for as soon as she declared to him in feeble words that she had changed her mind, and felt that she could not, dared not, fly with him, he forbore to urge her, grieved as he was at her decision. Unscrupulous pressure on his part, seeing how romantically she had become attached to him, would no doubt have turned the balance in his favour. But he did nothing to tempt her unduly or unfairly.

On her side, fearing for his safety, she begged him to remain. This, he declared, could not be. 'I cannot break faith with my friend,' said he. Had he stood alone he would have abandoned his plan. But Christoph, with the boat and compass and chart, was waiting on the shore; the tide would soon turn; his mother had been warned of his coming; go he must.

Many precious minutes were lost while he tarried, unable to tear himself away. Phyllis held to her resolve, though it cost her many a bitter pang. At last they parted, and he went down the hill. Before his footsteps had quite died away she felt a desire to behold at least his outline once more, and running noiselessly after him regained view of his diminishing figure. For one moment she was sufficiently excited to be on the point of rushing forward and linking her fate with his. But she could not. The courage which at the critical instant failed Cleopatra of Egypt could scarcely be expected of Phyllis Grove.

A dark shape, similar to his own, joined him in the highway. It was Christoph, his friend. She could see no more; they had hastened on in the direction of the town and harbour, four miles ahead. With a feeling akin to despair she turned and slowly pursued her way homeward.

Tattoo sounded in the camp; but there was no camp for her now. It was as dead as the camp of the Assyrians after the passage of the Destroying Angel.

She noiselessly entered the house, seeing nobody, and went to bed. Grief, which kept her awake at first, ultimately wrapped her in a heavy sleep. The next morning her father met her at the foot of the stairs.

'Mr Gould is come!' he said triumphantly.

Humphrey was staying at the inn, and had already called to inquire for her. He had brought her a present of a very handsome looking-glass in a frame of *repoussé* silverwork, which her father held in his hand. He had promised to call again in the course of an hour, to ask Phyllis to walk with him.

Pretty mirrors were rarer in country-houses at that day than they are now, and the one before her won Phyllis's admiration. She looked into it, saw how heavy her eyes were, and endeavoured to brighten them. She was in that wretched state of mind which leads a woman to move mechanically onward in what she conceives to be her allotted path. Mr Humphrey had, in his undemonstrative way, been adhering all along to the old understanding; it was for her to do the same, and to say not a word of her own lapse. She put on her bonnet and tippet, and when he arrived at the hour named she was at the door awaiting him.

V

Phyllis thanked him for his beautiful gift; but the talking was soon entirely on Humphrey's side as they walked along. He told her of the latest movements of the world of fashion – a subject which she willingly discussed to the exclusion of anything more personal – and his measured language helped to still her disquieted heart and brain. Had not her own sadness been what it was she must have observed his embarrassment. At last he abruptly changed the subject.

'I am glad you are pleased with my little present,' he said. 'The truth is that I brought it to propitiate 'ee, and to get you to help me out of a mighty difficulty.'

It was inconceivable to Phyllis that this independent bachelor – whom she admired in some respects – could have a difficulty.

'Phyllis – I'll tell you my secret at once; for I have a monstrous secret to confide before I can ask your counsel. The case is, then, that I am married: yes, I have privately married a dear young belle; and if you knew her, and I hope you will, you would say everything in her praise. But she is not quite the one that my father would have chose for me – you know the paternal idea as well as I – and I have kept it secret. There will be a terrible noise, no doubt; but I think that with your help I may get over it. If you would only do me this good turn – when I have told my father, I mean – say that you never could have married me, you know, or something of that sort – 'pon my life it will help to smooth the way vastly. I am so anxious to win him round to my point of view, and not to cause any estrangement.'

What Phyllis replied she scarcely knew, or how she counselled him as to his unexpected situation. Yet the relief that his announcement brought her was perceptible. To have confided her trouble in return was what her aching heart longed to do; and had Humphrey been a woman she would instantly have poured out her tale. But to him she feared to confess; and there was a real reason for silence, till a sufficient time had elapsed to allow her lover and his comrade to get out of harm's way.

As soon as she reached home again she sought a solitary place, and spent the time in half regretting that she had not gone away, and in dreaming over the meetings with Matthäus Tina from their beginning to their end. In his own country, amongst his own countrywomen, he would possibly soon forget her, even to her very name.

Her listlessness was such that she did not go out of the house for several days. There came a morning which broke in fog and mist, behind which the dawn could be discerned in greenish grey; and the outlines of the tents, and the rows of horses at the ropes. The smoke from the canteen fires drooped heavily.

The spot at the bottom of the garden where she had been accustomed to climb the wall to meet Matthäus, was the only inch of English ground in which she took any interest; and in spite of the disagreeable haze prevailing she walked out there till she reached the well-known corner. Every blade of grass was weighted with little liquid globes, and slugs and snails had crept out upon the plots. She could hear the usual faint noises from the camp, and in the other direction the trot of farmers on the road to the town, for it was market-day. She observed that her frequent visits to this corner had quite trodden down the grass in the angle of the wall, and left marks of garden soil on the stepping-stones by which she had mounted to look over the top. Seldom having gone there till dusk, she had not considered that her traces might be visible by day. Perhaps it was these which had revealed her trysts to her father.

While she paused in melancholy regard, she fancied that the customary sounds from the tents were changing their character. Indifferent as Phyllis was to camp doings now, she mounted by the steps to the old place. What she beheld at first awed and perplexed her; then she stood rigid, her fingers hooked to the wall, her eyes staring out of her head, and her face as if hardened to stone.

On the open green stretching before her all the regiments in the camp were drawn up in line, in the mid-front of which two empty coffins lay on the ground. The unwonted sounds which she had noticed came from an advancing procession. It consisted of the band of the York Hussars playing a dead march; next two soldiers of that regiment in a mourning coach, guarded on each side, and accompanied by two priests. Behind came a crowd of rustics who had been attracted by the event. The melancholy procession marched along the front of the line, returned to the centre, and halted beside the coffins, where the two condemned men were blind-folded, and each placed kneeling on his coffin; a few minutes' pause was now given, while they prayed.

A firing-party of twenty-four men stood ready with levelled carbines. The commanding officer, who had his sword drawn, waved it through some cuts of the sword-exercise till he reached the downward stroke, whereat the firing party discharged their volley. The two victims fell, one upon his face across his coffin, the other backwards.

As the volley resounded there arose a shriek from the wall of Dr Grove's garden, and some one fell down inside; but nobody among the spectators without noticed it at the time. The two executed Hussars were Matthäus Tina and his friend Christoph. The soldiers on guard placed the bodies in the coffins almost instantly; but the colonel of the regiment, an Englishman, rode up and exclaimed in a stern voice:

'Turn them out – as an example to the men!'

The coffins were lifted endwise, and the dead Germans flung out upon their faces on the grass. Then all the regiments wheeled in sections, and marched past the spot in slow time. When the survey was over the corpses were again coffined, and borne away.

Meanwhile Dr Grove, attracted by the noise of the volley, had rushed out into his garden, where he saw his wretched daughter lying motionless against the wall. She was taken indoors, but it was long before she recovered consciousness; and for weeks they despaired of her reason.

It transpired that the luckless deserters from the York Hussars had cut the boat from her moorings in the adjacent harbour, according to their plan, and, with two other comrades who were smarting under ill-treatment from their colonel, had sailed in safety across the Channel. But mistaking their bearings they steered into Jersey, thinking that island the French coast. Here they were perceived to be deserters, and delivered up to the authorities. Matthäus and Christoph interceded for the other two at the court-martial, saying that it was entirely by the former's representations that these were induced to go. Their sentence was accordingly commuted to flogging, the death punishment being reserved for their leaders.

The visitor to the well-known old Georgian wateringplace, who may care to ramble to the neighbouring village under the hills, and examine the register of burials, will there find two entries in these words:

Matth: Tina (Corpl.) in His Majesty's Regmt. of York Hussars, and Shot for Desertion, was Buried June 30th, 1801, aged 22 years. Born in the town of Sarrbruk, Germany.

Christoph Bless, belonging to His Majesty's Regmt. of York Hussars, who was Shot for Desertion, was Buried June 30th, 1801, aged 22 years. Born at Lothaargen, Alsatia.

Their graves were dug at the back of the little church, near the wall. There is no memorial to mark the spot, but Phyllis pointed it out to me. While she lived she used to keep their mounds neat; but now they are overgrown with nettles, and sunk nearly flat. The older villagers, however, who know of the episode from their parents, still recollect the place where the soldiers lie. Phyllis lies near.

THE DISTRACTED PREACHER

HOW HIS COLD WAS CURED

I

SOMETHING delayed the arrival of the Wesleyan minister, and a young man came temporarily in his stead. It was on the thirteenth of January 183– that Mr Stockdale, the young man in question, made his humble entry into the village, unknown, and almost unseen. But when those of the inhabitants who styled themselves of his connection became acquainted with him, they were rather pleased with the substitute than otherwise, though he had scarcely as yet acquired ballast of character sufficient to steady the consciences of the hundred-and-forty Methodists of pure blood who, at this time, lived in Nether-Moynton, and to give in addition supplementary support to the mixed race which went to church in the morning and chapel in the evening, or when there was a tea – as many as a hundred-and-ten people more, all told, and including the parish-clerk in the winter-time, when it was too dark for the vicar to observe who passed up the street at seven o'clock — which, to be just to him, he was never anxious to do.

It was owing to this overlapping of creeds that the celebrated population-puzzle arose among the denser gentry of the district around Nether-Moynton: how could it be that a parish containing fifteen score of strong full-grown Episcopalians, and nearly thirteen score of well-matured Dissenters, numbered barely two-and-twenty score adults in all?

The young man being personally interesting, those with whom he came in contact were content to waive for a while the graver question of his sufficiency. It is said that at this time of his life his eyes were affectionate, though without a ray of levity; that his hair was curly, and his figure tall; that he was, in short, a very lovable youth, who won upon his female hearers as soon as they saw and heard him, and caused them to say, 'Why didn't we know of this before he came, that we might have gi'ed him a warmer welcome!'

The fact was that, knowing him to be only provisionally selected, and expecting nothing remarkable in his person or doctrine, they and the rest of his flock in Nether-Moynton had felt almost as indifferent about his advent as if they had been the soundest church-going parishioners in the country, and he their true and appointed parson. Thus when Stockdale set foot in the place nobody had secured a lodging for him, and though his journey had given him a bad cold in the head he was forced to attend to that business himself. On inquiry he learnt that the only possible accommodation in the village would be found at the house of one Mrs Lizzy Newberry, at the upper end of the street.

It was a youth who gave this information, and Stockdale asked him who Mrs Newberry might be.

The boy said that she was a widow-woman, who had got no husband, because he was dead. Mr Newberry, he added, had been a well-to-do man enough, as the saying was, and a farmer; but he had gone off in a decline. As regarded Mrs Newberry's serious side, Stockdale gathered that she was one of the trimmers who went to church and chapel both.

'I'll go there,' said Stockdale, feeling that, in the absence of purely sectarian lodgings, he could do no better.

'She's a little particular, and wont hae gover'ment folks, or curates, or the pa'son's friends, or such like,' said the lad dubiously.

'Ah, that may be a promising sign: I'll call. Or no; just you go up and ask first if she can find room for me. I have to see one or two persons on another matter. You will find me down at the carrier's.'

In a quarter of an hour the lad came back, and said that Mrs Newberry would have no objection to accommodate him, whereupon Stockdale called at the house. It stood within a garden-hedge, and seemed to be roomy and comfortable. He saw an elderly woman, with whom he made arrangements to come the same night, since there was no inn in the place, and he wished to house himself as soon as possible; the village being a local centre from which he was to radiate at once to the different small chapels in the neighbourhood. He forthwith sent his luggage to Mrs Newberry's from the carrier's, where he had taken shelter, and in the evening walked up to his temporary home.

As he now lived there, Stockdale felt it unnecessary to knock at the door; and entering quietly he had the pleasure of hearing footsteps scudding away like mice into the back quarters. He advanced to the parlour, as the front room was called, though its stone floor was scarcely disguised by the carpet, which only overlaid the trodden areas, leaving sandy deserts under the furniture. But the room looked snug and cheerful. The firelight shone out brightly, trembling on the bulging mouldings of the table-legs, playing with brass knobs and handles, and lurking in great strength on the under surface of the chimney-piece. A deep arm-chair, covered with horsehair, and studded with a countless throng of brass nails, was pulled up on one side of the fireplace. The tea-things were on the table, the teapot cover was open, and a little handbell had been laid at that precise point towards which a person seated in the great chair might be expected instinctively to stretch his hand.

Stockdale sat down, not objecting to his experience of the room thus far, and began his residence by tinkling the bell. A little girl crept in at the summons, and made tea for him. Her name, she said, was Marther Sarer, and she lived out there, nodding towards the road and village generally. Before Stockdale had got far with his meal a tap sounded on the door behind him, and on his telling the inquirer to come in, a rustle of garments caused him to turn his head. He saw before him a fine and extremely well-made young woman, with dark hair, a wide, sensible, beautiful forehead, eyes that warmed him before he knew it, and a mouth that was in itself a picture to all appreciative souls.

'Can I get you anything else for tea?' she said, coming forward a step or two, an expression of liveliness on her features, and her hand waving the door by its edge.

'Nothing, thank you,' said Stockdale, thinking less of what he replied than of what might be her relation to the household.

'You are quite sure?' said the young woman, apparently aware that he had not considered his answer.

He conscientiously examined the tea-things, and found them all there. 'Quite sure, Miss Newberry,' he said.

'It is Mrs Newberry,' she said. 'Lizzy Newberry. I used to be Lizzy Simpkins.'

'O, I beg your pardon, Mrs Newberry.' And before he had occasion to say more she left the room.

Stockdale remained in some doubt till Martha Sarah came to clear the table. 'Whose house is this, my little woman?' said he.

'Mrs Lizzy Newberry's, sir.'

'Then Mrs Newberry is not the old lady I saw this afternoon?'

'No. That's Mrs Newberry's mother. It was Mrs Newberry who comed in to you just by now, because she wanted to see if you was good-looking.'

Later in the evening, when Stockdale was about to begin supper, she came again. 'I have come myself, Mr Stockdale,' she said. The minister stood up in acknowledgment of the honour. 'I am afraid little Martha might not make you understand. What will you have for supper? – there's cold rabbit, and there's a ham uncut.'

Stockdale said he could get on nicely with those viands, and supper was laid. He had no more than cut a slice when tap-tap came to the door again. The minister had already learnt that this particular rhythm in taps denoted the fingers of his enkindling landlady, and the doomed young fellow buried his first mouthful under a look of receptive blandness.

'We have a chicken in the house, Mr Stockdale – I quite forgot to mention it just now. Perhaps you would like Marther Sarer to bring it up?'

Stockdale had advanced far enough in the art of being a young man to say that he did not want the chicken, unless she brought it up herself; but when it was uttered he blushed at the daring gallantry of the speech, perhaps a shade too strong for a serious man and a minister. In three minutes the chicken appeared, but, to his great surprise, only in the hands of Martha Sarah. Stockdale was disappointed, which perhaps it was intended that he should be.

He had finished supper, and was not in the least anticipating Mrs Newberry again that night, when she tapped and entered as before. Stockdale's gratified look told that she had lost nothing by not appearing when expected. It happened that the cold in the head from which the young man suffered had increased with the approach of night, and before she had spoken he was seized with a violent fit of sneezing which he could not anyhow repress.

Mrs Newberry looked full of pity. 'Your cold is very bad to-night, Mr Stockdale.'

Stockdale replied that it was rather troublesome.

'And I've a good mind –' she added archly, looking at the cheerless glass of water on the table, which the abstemious minister was going to drink.

'Yes, Mrs Newberry?'

'I've a good mind that you should have something more likely to cure it than that cold stuff.'

'Well,' said Stockdale, looking down at the glass, 'as there is no inn here, and nothing better to be got in the village, of course it will do.'

To this she replied, 'There is something better, not far off, though not in the house. I really think you must try it, or

you may be ill. Yes, Mr Stockdale, you shall.' She held up
her finger, seeing that he was about to speak. 'Don't ask
what it is; wait, and you shall see.'

Lizzy went away, and Stockdale waited in a pleasant
mood. Presently she returned with her bonnet and cloak on,
saying, 'I am so sorry, but you must help me to get it.
Mother has gone to bed. Will you wrap yourself up, and
come this way, and please bring that cup with you?'

Stockdale, a lonely young fellow, who had for weeks felt a
great craving for somebody on whom to throw away
superfluous interest, and even tenderness, was not sorry to
join her; and followed his guide through the back door,
across the garden, to the bottom, where the boundary was a
wall. This wall was low, and beyond it Stockdale discerned
in the night shades several grey headstones, and the outlines
of the church roof and tower.

'It is easy to get up this way,' she said, stepping upon a
bank which abutted on the wall; then putting her foot on the
top of the stonework, and descending by a spring inside,
where the ground was much higher, as is the manner of
graveyards to be. Stockdale did the same, and followed her
in the dusk across the irregular ground till they came to the
tower door, which, when they had entered, she softly closed
behind them.

'You can keep a secret?' she said, in a musical voice.

'Like an iron chest!' said he fervently.

Then from under her cloak she produced a small lighted
lantern, which the minister had not noticed that she carried
at all. The light showed them to be close to the singing-
gallery stairs, under which lay a heap of lumber of all sorts,
but consisting mostly of decayed framework, pews, panels,
and pieces of flooring, that from time to time had been
removed from their original fixings in the body of the edifice
and replaced by new.

'Perhaps you will drag some of those boards aside?' she
said, holding the lantern over her head to light him better.

'Or will you take the lantern while I move them?'

'I can manage it,' said the young man, and acting as she ordered, he uncovered, to his surprise, a row of little barrels bound with wood hoops, each barrel being about as large as the nave of a heavy waggon-wheel. When they were laid open Lizzy fixed her eyes on him, as if she wondered what he would say.

'You know what they are?' she asked, finding that he did not speak.

'Yes, barrels,' said Stockdale simply. He was an inland man, the son of highly respectable parents, and brought up with a single eye to the ministry; and the sight suggested nothing beyond the fact that such articles were there.

'You are quite right, they are barrels,' she said, in an emphatic tone of candour that was not without a touch of irony.

Stockdale looked at her with an eye of sudden misgiving. 'Not smugglers' liquor?' he said.

'Yes,' said she. 'They are tubs of spirit that have accidentally floated over in the dark from France.'

In Nether-Moynton and its vicinity at this date people always smiled at the sort of sin called in the outside world illicit trading; and these little kegs of gin and brandy were as well known to the inhabitants as turnips. So that Stockdale's innocent ignorance, and his look of alarm when he guessed the sinister mystery, seemed to strike Lizzy first as ludicrous, and then as very awkward for the good impression that she wished to produce upon him.

'Smuggling is carried on here by some of the people,' she said in a gentle, apologetic voice. 'It has been their practice for generations, and they think it no harm. Now, will you roll out one of the tubs?'

'What to do with it?' said the minister.

'To draw a little from it to cure your cold,' she answered. 'It is so 'nation strong that it drives away that sort of thing in a jiffy. O, it is all right about our taking it. I may have what

I like; the owner of the tubs says so. I ought to have had some in the house, and then I shouldn't ha' been put to this trouble; but I drink none myself, and so I often forget to keep it indoors.'

'You are allowed to help yourself, I suppose, that you may not inform where their hiding-place is?'

'Well, no; not that particularly; but I may take any if I want it. So help yourself.'

'I will, to oblige you, since you have a right to it,' murmured the minister; and though he was not quite satisfied with his part in the performance, he rolled one of the 'tubs' out from the corner into the middle of the tower floor. 'How do you wish me to get it out – with a gimlet, I suppose?'

'No, I'll show you,' said his interesting companion; and she held up with her other hand a shoemaker's awl and a hammer. 'You must never do these things with a gimlet, because the wood-dust gets in; and when the buyers pour out the brandy that would tell them that the tub had been broached. An awl makes no dust, and the hole nearly closes up again. Now tap one of the hoops forward.'

Stockdale took the hammer and did so.

'Now make the hole in the part that was covered by the hoop.'

He made the hole as directed. 'It won't run out,' he said.

'O yes it will,' said she. 'Take the tub between your knees, and squeeze the heads; and I'll hold the cup.'

Stockdale obeyed; and the pressure taking effect upon the tub, which seemed to be thin, the spirit spurted out in a stream. When the cup was full he ceased pressing, and the flow immediately stopped. 'Now we must fill up the keg with water,' said Lizzy, 'or it will cluck like forty hens when it is handled, and show that 'tis not full.'

'But they tell you you may take it?'

'Yes, the *smugglers*; but the *buyers* must not know that the smugglers have been kind to me at their expense.'

'I see,' said Stockdale doubtfully. 'I must question the honesty of this proceeding.'

By her direction he held the tub with the hole upwards, and while he went through the process of alternately pressing and ceasing to press, she produced a bottle of water, from which she took mouthfuls, conveying each to the keg by putting her pretty lips to the hole, where it was sucked in at each recovery of the cask from pressure. When it was again full he plugged the hole, knocked the hoop down to its place, and buried the tub in the lumber as before.

'Aren't the smugglers afraid that you will tell?' he asked, as they recrossed the churchyard.

'O no; they are not afraid of that. I couldn't do such a thing.'

'They have put you into a very awkward corner,' said Stockdale emphatically. 'You must, of course, as an honest person, sometimes feel that it is your duty to inform – really you must.'

'Well, I have never particularly felt it as a duty; and, besides, my first husband –' She stopped, and there was some confusion in her voice. Stockdale was so honest and unsophisticated that he did not at once discern why she paused: but at last he did perceive that the words were a slip, and that no woman would have uttered 'first husband' by accident unless she had thought pretty frequently of a second. He felt for her confusion, and allowed her time to recover and proceed. 'My husband,' she said, in a self-corrected tone, 'used to know of their doings, and so did my father, and kept the secret. I cannot inform, in fact, against anybody.'

'I see the hardness of it,' he continued, like a man who looked far into the moral of things. 'And it is very cruel that you should be tossed and tantalized between your memories and your conscience. I do hope, Mrs Newberry, that you will soon see your way out of this unpleasant position.'

'Well, I don't just now,' she murmured.

By this time they had passed over the wall and entered the house, where she brought him a glass and hot water, and left him to his own reflections. He looked after her vanishing form, asking himself whether he, as a respectable man, and a minister, and a shining light, even though as yet only of the halfpenny-candle sort, were quite justified in doing this thing. A sneeze settled the question; and he found that when the fiery liquor was lowered by the addition of twice or thrice the quantity of water, it was one of the prettiest cures for a cold in the head that he had ever known, particularly at this chilly time of the year.

Stockdale sat in the deep chair about twenty minutes sipping and meditating, till he at length took warmer views of things, and longed for the morrow, when he would see Mrs Newberry again. He then felt that, though chronologically at a short distance, it would in an emotional sense be very long before to-morrow came, and walked restlessly round the room. His eye was attracted by a framed and glazed sampler in which a running ornament of fir-trees and peacocks surrounded the following pretty bit of sentiment:

> Rose-leaves smell when roses thrive,
> Here's my work while I'm alive;
> Rose-leaves smell when shrunk and shed,
> Here's my work when I am dead.

Lizzy Simpkins.   Fear God.   Honour the King.
Aged 11 years.

' 'Tis hers,' he said to himself. 'Heavens, how I like that name!'

Before he had done thinking that no other name from Abigail to Zenobia would have suited his young landlady so well, tap-tap came again upon the door; and the minister started as her face appeared yet another time, looking so disinterested that the most ingenious would have refrained

from asserting that she had come to affect his feelings by her
seductive eyes.

'Would you like a fire in your room, Mr Stockdale, on
account of your cold?'

The minister, being a little pricked in the conscience for
countenancing her in watering the spirits, saw here a way to
self-chastisement. 'No, I thank you,' he said firmly; 'it is
not necessary. I have never been used to one in my life, and
it would be giving way to luxury too far.'

'Then I won't insist,' she said, and disconcerted him by
vanishing instantly.

Wondering if she was vexed by his refusal, he wished that
he had chosen to have a fire, even though it should have
scorched him out of bed and endangered his self-discipline
for a dozen days. However, he consoled himself with what
was in truth a rare consolation for a budding lover, that he
was under the same roof with Lizzy; her guest, in fact, to
take a poetical view of the term lodger; and that he would
certainly see her on the morrow.

The morrow came, and Stockdale rose early, his cold
quite gone. He had never in his life so longed for the breakfast hour as he did that day, and punctually at eight o'clock,
after a short walk to reconnoitre the premises, he re-entered
the door of his dwelling. Breakfast passed, and Martha
Sarah attended, but nobody came voluntarily as on the
night before to inquire if there were other wants which he
had not mentioned, and which she would attempt to gratify.
He was disappointed, and went out, hoping to see her at
dinner. Dinner time came; he sat down to the meal, finished
it, lingered on for a whole hour, although two new teachers
were at that moment waiting at the chapel-door to speak to
him by appointment. It was useless to wait longer, and he
slowly went his way down the lane, cheered by the thought
that, after all, he would see her in the evening, and perhaps
engage again in the delightful tub-broaching in the neighbouring church tower, which proceeding he resolved to

render more moral by steadfastly insisting that no water should be introduced to fill up, though the tub should cluck like all the hens in Christendom. But nothing could disguise the fact that it was a queer business; and his countenance fell when he thought how much more his mind was interested in that matter than in his serious duties.

However, compunction vanished with the decline of day. Night came, and his tea and supper; but no Lizzy Newberry, and no sweet temptations. At last the minister could bear it no longer, and said to his quaint little attendant, 'Where is Mrs Newberry to-day?' judiciously handing a penny as he spoke.

'She's busy,' said Martha.

'Anything serious happened?' he asked, handing another penny, and revealing yet additional pennies in the background.

'O no – nothing at all!' said she, with breathless confidence. 'Nothing ever happens to her. She's only biding upstairs in bed because 'tis her way sometimes.'

Being a young man of some honour he would not question further, and assuming that Lizzy must have a bad headache, or other slight ailment, in spite of what the girl had said, he went to bed dissatisfied, not even setting eyes on old Mrs Simpkins. 'I said last night that I should see her to-morrow,' he reflected; 'but that was not to be!'

Next day he had better fortune, or worse, meeting her at the foot of the stairs in the morning, and being favoured by a visit or two from her during the day – once for the purpose of making kindly inquiries about his comfort, as on the first evening, and at another time to place a bunch of winter-violets on his table, with a promise to renew them when they drooped. On these occasions there was something in her smile which showed how conscious she was of the effect she produced, though it must be said that it was rather a humorous than a designing consciousness, and savoured more of pride than of vanity.

As for Stockdale, he clearly perceived that he possessed unlimited capacity for backsliding, and wished that tutelary saints were not denied to Dissenters. He set a watch upon his tongue and eyes for the space of one hour and a half, after which he found it was useless to struggle further, and gave himself up to the situation. 'The other minister will be here in a month,' he said to himself when sitting over the fire. 'Then I shall be off, and she will distract my mind no more! . . . And then, shall I go on living by myself for ever? No; when my two years of probation are finished, I shall have a furnished house to live in, with a varnished door and a brass knocker; and I'll march straight back to her, and ask her flat, as soon as the last plate is on the dresser!'

Thus a titillating fortnight was passed by young Stockdale, during which time things proceeded much as such matters have done ever since the beginning of history. He saw the object of attachment several times one day, did not see her at all the next, met her when he least expected to do so, missed her when hints and signs as to where she should be at a given hour almost amounted to an appointment. This mild coquetry was perhaps fair enough under the circumstances of their being so closely lodged, and Stockdale put up with it as philosophically as he was able. Being in her own house she could, after vexing him or disappointing him of her presence, easily win him back by suddenly surrounding him with those little attentions which her position as his landlady put it in her power to bestow. When he had waited indoors half the day to see her, and on finding that she would not be seen, had gone off in a huff to the dreariest and dampest walk he could discover, she would restore equilibrium in the evening with 'Mr Stockdale, I have fancied you must feel draught o' nights from your bedroom window, and so I have been putting up thicker curtains this afternoon while you were out'; or, 'I noticed that you sneezed twice again this morning, Mr Stockdale. Depend upon it that cold is hanging about you yet; I am sure it is – I have thought of it continually; and you must let me make a posset for you.'

Sometimes in coming home he found his sitting-room re-arranged, chairs placed where the table had stood, and the table ornamented with a few fresh flowers and leaves that could be obtained at this season, so as to add a novelty to the room. At times she would be standing on a chair outside the house, trying to nail up a branch of the monthly rose which the winter wind had blown down; and of course he stepped forward to assist her, when their hands got mixed in passing the shreds and nails. Thus they became friends again after a disagreement. She would utter on these occasions some pretty and deprecatory remark on the necessity of her troubling him anew; and he would straightway say that he would do a hundred times as much for her if she should so require.

HOW HE SAW TWO OTHER MEN

II

Matters being in this advancing state, Stockdale was rather surprised one cloudy evening, while sitting in his room, at hearing her speak in low tones of expostulation to some one at the door. It was nearly dark, but the shutters were not yet closed, nor the candles lighted; and Stockdale was tempted to stretch his head towards the window. He saw outside the door a young man in clothes of a whitish colour, and upon reflection judged their wearer to be the well-built and rather handsome miller who lived below. The miller's voice was alternately low and firm, and sometimes it reached the level of positive entreaty; but what the words were Stockdale could in no way hear.

Before the colloquy had ended, the minister's attention was attracted by a second incident. Opposite Lizzy's home grew a clump of laurels, forming a thick and permanent shade. One of the laurel boughs now quivered against the light background of sky, and in a moment the head of a man peered out, and remained still. He seemed to be also much interested in the conversation at the door, and was plainly lingering there to watch and listen. Had Stockdale stood in any other relation to Lizzy than that of a lover, he might have gone out and investigated the meaning of this: but being as yet but an unprivileged ally, he did nothing more than stand up and show himself against the firelight, where-upon the listener disappeared, and Lizzy and the miller spoke in lower tones.

Stockdale was made so uneasy by the circumstance, that as soon as the miller was gone, he said, 'Mrs Newberry, are you aware that you were watched just now, and your conversation heard?'

'When?' she said.

'When you were talking to that miller. A man was looking from the laurel-tree as jealously as if he could have eaten you.'

She showed more concern than the trifling event seemed to demand, and he added, 'Perhaps you were talking of things you did not wish to be overheard?'

'I was talking only on business,' she said.

'Lizzy, be frank!' said the young man. 'If it was only on business, why should anybody wish to listen to you?'

She looked curiously at him. 'What else do you think it could be, then?'

'Well – the only talk between a young woman and man that is likely to amuse an eavesdropper.'

'Ah yes,' she said, smiling in spite of her preoccupation. 'Well, my cousin Owlett has spoken to me about matri-mony, every now and then, that's true; but he was not speaking of it then. I wish he had been speaking of it, with all my heart. It would have been much less serious for me.'

'O Mrs Newberry!'

'It would. Not that I should ha' chimed in with him, of

course. I wish it for other reasons. I am glad, Mr Stockdale, that you have told me of that listener. It is a timely warning, and I must see my cousin again.'

'But don't go away till I have spoken,' said the minister. 'I'll out with it at once, and make no more ado. Let it be Yes or No between us, Lizzy; please do!' And he held out his hand, in which she freely allowed her own to rest, but without speaking.

'You mean Yes by that?' he asked, after waiting a while.

'You may be my sweetheart, if you will.'

'Why not say at once you will wait for me until I have a house and can come back to marry you.'

'Because I am thinking – thinking of something else,' she said with embarrassment. 'It all comes upon me at once, and I must settle one thing at a time.'

'At any rate, dear Lizzy, you can assure me that the miller shall not be allowed to speak to you except on business? You have never directly encouraged him?'

She parried the question by saying, 'You see, he and his party have been in the habit of leaving things on my premises sometimes, and as I have not denied him, it makes him rather forward.'

'Things – what things?'

'Tubs – they are called Things here.'

'But why don't you deny him, my dear Lizzy?'

'I cannot well.'

'You are too timid. It is unfair of him to impose so upon you, and get your good name into danger by his smuggling tricks. Promise me that the next time he wants to leave his tubs here you will let me roll them into the street?'

She shook her head. 'I would not venture to offend the neighbours so much as that,' said she, 'or do anything that would be so likely to put poor Owlett into the hands of the Customs-men.'

Stockdale sighed, and said that he thought hers a mistaken generosity when it extended to assisting those who cheated the king of his dues. 'At any rate, you will let me make him keep his distance as your lover, and tell him flatly that you are not for him?'

'Please not, at present,' she said. 'I don't wish to offend my old neighbours. It is not only Mr Owlett who is concerned.'

'This is too bad,' said Stockdale impatiently.

'On my honour, I won't encourage him as my lover,' Lizzy answered earnestly. 'A reasonable man will be satisfied with that.'

'Well, so I am,' said Stockdale, his countenance clearing.

THE MYSTERIOUS GREATCOAT

III

Stockdale now began to notice more particularly a feature in the life of his fair landlady, which he had casually observed but scarcely ever thought of before. It was that she was markedly irregular in her hours of rising. For a week or two she would be tolerably punctual, reaching the ground-floor within a few minutes of half-past seven. Then suddenly she would not be visible till twelve at noon, perhaps for three or four days in succession; and twice he had certain proof that she did not leave her room till half-past three in the afternoon. The second time that this extreme lateness came under his notice was on a day when he had particularly wished to consult with her about his future movements; and he concluded, as he always had done, that she had a cold, headache, or other ailment, unless she had kept herself invisible to avoid meeting and talking to him, which he could hardly believe. The former supposition was disproved, however, by her innocently saying, some days later, when they were speaking on a question of health, that she had never had a moment's heaviness, headache, or illness of any kind since the previous January twelve-month.

'I am glad to hear it,' said he. 'I thought quite otherwise.'

'What, do I look sickly?' she asked, turning up her face to show the impossibility of his gazing on it and holding such a belief for a moment.

'Not at all; I merely thought so from your being sometimes obliged to keep your room through the best part of the day.'

'O, as for that – it means nothing,' she murmured, with a look which some might have called cold, and which was the worst look that he liked to see upon her. 'It is pure sleepiness, Mr Stockdale.'

'Never!'

'It is, I tell you. When I stay in my room till half-past three in the afternoon, you may always be sure that I slept soundly till three, or I shouldn't have stayed there.'

'It is dreadful,' said Stockdale, thinking of the disastrous effects of such indulgence upon the household of a minister, should it become a habit of everyday occurrence.

'But then,' she said, divining his good and prescient thoughts, 'it only happens when I stay awake all night. I don't go to sleep till five or six in the morning sometimes.'

'Ah, that's another matter,' said Stockdale. 'Sleeplessness to such an alarming extent is real illness. Have you spoken to a doctor?'

'O no – there is no need for doing that – it is all natural to me.' And she went away without further remark.

Stockdale might have waited a long time to know the real cause of her sleeplessness, had it not happened that one dark night he was sitting in his bedroom jotting down notes for a sermon, which occupied him perfunctorily for a considerable time after the other members of the household had retired. He did not get to bed till one o'clock. Before he had fallen asleep he heard a knocking at the front door, first rather timidly performed, and then louder. Nobody answered it, and the person knocked again. As the house still remained undisturbed, Stockdale got out of bed, went to his window, which overlooked the door, and opening it, asked who was there.

A young woman's voice replied that Susan Wallis was there, and that she had come to ask if Mrs Newberry could give her some mustard to make a plaster with, as her father was taken very ill on the chest.

The minister, having neither bell nor servant, was compelled to act in person. 'I will call Mrs Newberry,' he said. Partly dressing himself, he went along the passage and tapped at Lizzy's door. She did not answer, and, thinking of her erratic habits in the matter of sleep, he thumped the door persistently, when he discovered, by its moving ajar under his knocking, that it had only been gently pushed to. As there was now a sufficient entry for the voice, he knocked no longer, but said in firm tones, 'Mrs Newberry, you are wanted.'

The room was quite silent; not a breathing, not a rustle, came from any part of it. Stockdale now sent a positive shout through the open space of the door: 'Mrs Newberry!' – still no answer, or movement of any kind within. Then he heard sounds from the opposite room, that of Lizzy's mother, as if she had been aroused by his uproar though Lizzy had not, and was dressing herself hastily. Stockdale softly closed the younger woman's door and went on to the other, which was opened by Mrs Simpkins before he could reach it. She was in her ordinary clothes, and had a light in her hand.

'What's the person calling about?' she said in alarm.

Stockdale told the girl's errand, adding seriously, 'I cannot wake Mrs Newberry.'

'It is no matter,' said her mother. 'I can let the girl have what she wants as well as my daughter.' And she came out of the room and went downstairs.

Stockdale retired towards his own apartment, saying, however, to Mrs Simpkins from the landing, as if on second thoughts, 'I suppose there is nothing the matter with Mrs

Newberry, that I could not wake her?'

'O no,' said the old lady hastily. 'Nothing at all.'

Still the minister was not satisfied. 'Will you go in and see?' he said. 'I should be much more at ease.'

Mrs Simpkins returned up the staircase, went to her daughter's room, and came out again almost instantly. 'There is nothing at all the matter with Lizzy,' she said; and descended again to attend to the applicant, who, having seen the light, had remained quiet during this interval.

Stockdale went into his room and lay down as before. He heard Lizzy's mother open the front door, admit the girl, and then the murmured discourse of both as they went to the store-cupboard for the medicament required. The girl departed, the door was fastened, Mrs Simpkins came upstairs, and the house was again in silence. Still the minister did not fall asleep. He could not get rid of a singular suspicion, which was all the more harassing in being, if true, the most unaccountable thing within his experience. That Lizzy Newberry was in her bedroom when he made such a clamour at the door he could not possibly convince himself, notwithstanding that he had heard her come upstairs at the usual time, go into her chamber, and shut herself up in the usual way. Yet all reason was so much against her being elsewhere, that he was constrained to go back again to the unlikely theory of a heavy sleep, though he had heard neither breath nor movement during a shouting and knocking loud enough to rouse the Seven Sleepers.

Before coming to any positive conclusion he fell asleep himself, and did not awake till day. He saw nothing of Mrs Newberry in the morning, before he went out to meet the rising sun, as he liked to do when the weather was fine; but as this was by no means unusual, he took no notice of it. At breakfast-time he knew that she was not far off by hearing her in the kitchen, and though he saw nothing of her person, that back apartment being rigorously closed against his eyes, she seemed to be talking, ordering, and bustling about among the pots and skimmers in so ordinary a manner, that there was no reason for his wasting more time in fruitless surmise.

The minister suffered from these distractions, and his extemporized sermons were not improved thereby. Already he often said Romans for Corinthians in the pulpit, and gave out hymns in strange cramped metres, that hitherto had always been skipped, because the congregation could not raise a tune to fit them. He fully resolved that as soon as his few weeks of stay approached their end he would cut the matter short, and commit himself by proposing a definite engagement, repenting at leisure if necessary.

With this end in view, he suggested to her on the evening after her mysterious sleep that they should take a walk together just before dark, the latter part of the proposition being introduced that they might return home unseen. She consented to go; and away they went over a stile, to a shrouded footpath suited for the occasion. But, in spite of attempts on both sides, they were unable to infuse much spirit into the ramble. She looked rather paler than usual, and sometimes turned her head away.

'Lizzy,' said Stockdale reproachfully, when they had walked in silence a long distance.

'Yes,' said she.

'You yawned – much my company is to you!' He put it in that way, but he was really wondering whether her yawn could possibly have more to do with physical weariness from the night before than mental weariness of that present moment. Lizzy apologized, and owned that she was rather tired, which gave him an opening for a direct question on the point; but his modesty would not allow him to put it to her; and he uncomfortably resolved to wait.

The month of February passed with alternations of mud and frost, rain and sleet, east winds and north-westerly gales. The hollow places in the ploughed fields showed themselves as pools of water, which had settled there from the higher levels, and had not yet found time to soak away. The birds began to get lively, and a single thrush came just before sunset each evening, and sang hopefully on the large elm-tree which stood nearest to Mrs Newberry's house. Cold blasts and brittle earth had given place to an oozing dampness more unpleasant in itself than frost; but it suggested coming spring, and its unpleasantness was of a bearable kind.

Stockdale had been going to bring about a practical understanding with Lizzy at least half a dozen times; but, what with the mystery of her apparent absence on the night of the neighbour's call, and her curious way of lying in bed at unaccountable times, he felt a check within him whenever he wanted to speak out. Thus they still lived on as indefinitely affianced lovers, each of whom hardly acknowledged the other's claim to the name of chosen one. Stockdale persuaded himself that his hesitation was owing to the postponement of the ordained minister's arrival, and the consequent delay in his own departure, which did away with all necessity for haste in his courtship; but perhaps it was only that his discretion was reasserting itself, and telling him that he had better get clearer ideas of Lizzy before arranging for the grand contract of his life with her. She, on her part, always seemed ready to be urged further on that question than he had hitherto attempted to go; but she was none the less independent, and to a degree which would have kept from flagging the passion of a far more mutable man.

On the evening of the first of March he went casually into his bedroom about dusk, and noticed lying on a chair a greatcoat, hat, and breeches. Having no recollection of leaving any clothes of his own in this spot, he went and examined them as well as he could in the twilight, and found that they did not belong to him. He paused for a moment to consider how they might have got there. He was the only man living in the house; and yet these were not his garments, unless he had made a mistake. No, they were not his. He called up Martha Sarah.

'How did these things come in my room?' he said, flinging the objectionable articles to the floor.

Martha said that Mrs Newberry had given them to her to brush, and that she had brought them up there thinking they must be Mr Stockdale's, as there was no other gentleman a-lodging there.

'Of course you did,' said Stockdale. 'Now take them down to your mis'ess, and say they are some clothes I have found here and know nothing about.'

As the door was left open he heard the conversation downstairs. 'How stupid!' said Mrs Newberry, in a tone of confusion. 'Why, Marther Sarer, I did not tell you to take 'em to Mr Stockdale's room?'

'I thought they must be his as they was so muddy,' said Martha humbly.

'You should have left 'em on the clothes-horse,' said the young mistress severely; and she came upstairs with the garments on her arm, quickly passed Stockdale's room, and threw them forcibly into a closet at the end of a passage. With this the incident ended, and the house was silent again.

There would have been nothing remarkable in finding such clothes in a widow's house had they been clean; or moth-eaten, or creased, or mouldy from long lying by; but that they should be splashed with recent mud bothered Stockdale a good deal. When a young pastor is in the aspen stage of attachment, and open to agitation at the merest trifles, a really substantial incongruity of this complexion is a disturbing thing. However, nothing further occurred at that time; but he became watchful, and given to conjecture, and was unable to forget the circumstance.

One morning, on looking from his window, he saw Mrs Newberry herself brushing the tails of a long drab greatcoat, which, if he mistook not, was the very same garment as the one that had adorned the chair of his room. It was densely splashed up to the hollow of the back with neighbouring Nether-Moynton mud, to judge by its colour, the spots being distinctly visible to him in the sunlight. The previous day or two having been wet, the inference was irresistible that the wearer had quite recently been walking some considerable distance about the lanes and fields. Stockdale opened the window and looked out, and Mrs Newberry turned her head. Her face became slowly red; she never had looked prettier, or more incomprehensible. He waved his hand affectionately, and said good-morning; she answered with embarrassment, having ceased her occupation on the instant that she saw him, and rolled up the coat half-cleaned.

Stockdale shut the window. Some simple explanation of her proceeding was doubtless within the bounds of possibility; but he himself could not think of one; and he wished that she had placed the matter beyond conjecture by voluntarily saying something about it there and then.

But, though Lizzy had not offered an explanation at the moment, the subject was brought forward by her at the next time of their meeting. She was chatting to him concerning some other event, and remarked that it happened about the time when she was dusting some old clothes that had belonged to her poor husband.

'You keep them clean out of respect to his memory?' said Stockdale tentatively.

'I air and dust them sometimes,' she said, with the most charming innocence in the world.

'Do dead men come out of their graves and walk in mud?' murmured the minister, in a cold sweat at the deception that she was practising.

'What did you say?' asked Lizzy.

'Nothing, nothing,' said he mournfully. 'Mere words – a phrase that will do for my sermon next Sunday.' It was too plain that Lizzy was unaware that he had seen fresh pedestrian splashes upon the skirts of the tell-tale overcoat, and that she imagined him to believe it had come direct from some chest or drawer.

The aspect of the case was now considerably darker. Stockdale was so much depressed by it that he did not challenge her explanation, or threaten to go off as a missionary to benighted islanders, or reproach her in any way whatever. He simply parted from her when she had done talking, and lived on in perplexity, till by degrees his natural manner became sad and constrained.

AT THE TIME OF THE NEW MOON

IV

The following Thursday was changeable, damp, and gloomy; and the night threatened to be windy and unpleasant. Stockdale had gone away to Knollsea in the morning, to be present at some commemoration service there, and on his return he was met by the attractive Lizzy in the passage. Whether influenced by the tide of cheerfulness which had attended him that day, or by the drive through the open air, or whether from a natural disposition to let bygones alone, he allowed himself to be fascinated into forgetfulness of the greatcoat incident, and upon the whole passed a pleasant evening; not so much in her society as within sound of her voice, as she sat talking in the back parlour to her mother, till the latter went to bed. Shortly after this Mrs Newberry retired, and then Stockdale prepared to go upstairs himself. But before he left the room he remained standing by the dying embers awhile, thinking long of one thing and another; and was only aroused by the flickering of his candle in the socket as it suddenly declined and went out. Knowing that there were a tinder-box, matches, and another candle in his bedroom, he felt his way upstairs without a light. On reaching his chamber he laid his hand on every possible ledge and corner for the tinder-box, but for a long time in vain. Discovering it at length, Stockdale produced a spark, and was kindling the brimstone, when he fancied that he heard a movement in the passage. He blew harder at the lint, the match flared up, and looking by aid of the blue light through the door, which had been standing open all this time, he was surprised to see a male figure vanishing round the top of the staircase with the evident intention of escaping unobserved. The personage wore the clothes which Lizzy had been brushing, and something in the outline and gait suggested to the minister that the wearer was Lizzy herself.

But he was not sure of this; and, greatly excited, Stockdale determined to investigate the mystery, and to adopt his own way for doing it. He blew out the match without lighting the candle, went into the passage, and proceeded on tiptoe towards Lizzy's room. A faint grey square of light in the direction of the chamber-window as he approached told him that the door was open, and at once suggested that the occupant was gone. He turned and brought down his fist upon the handrail of the staircase: 'It was she; in her late husband's coat and hat!'

Somewhat relieved to find that there was no intruder in the case, yet none the less surprised, the minister crept down the stairs, softly put on his boots, overcoat, and hat, and tried the front door. It was fastened as usual: he went to the back door, found this unlocked, and emerged into the garden. The night was mild and moonless, and rain had lately been falling, though for the present it had ceased. There was a sudden dropping from the trees and bushes every now and then, as each passing wind shook their boughs. Among these sounds Stockdale heard the faint fall of feet upon the road outside, and he guessed from the step that it was Lizzy's. He followed the sound, and, helped by the circumstance of the wind blowing from the direction in which the pedestrian moved, he got nearly close to her, and

kept there, without risk of being overheard. While he thus
followed her up the street or lane, as it might indifferently be
called, there being more hedge than houses on either side, a
figure came forward to her from one of the cottage doors.
Lizzy stopped; the minister stepped upon the grass and
stopped also.

'Is that Mrs Newberry?' said the man who had come out,
whose voice Stockdale recognized as that of one of the most
devout members of his congregation.

'It is,' said Lizzy.

'I be quite ready – I've been here this quarter-hour.'

'Ah, John,' said she, 'I have bad news; there is danger
tonight for our venture.'

'And d'ye tell o't! I dreamed there might be.'

'Yes,' she said hurriedly; 'and you must go at once round
to where the chaps are waiting, and tell them they will not
be wanted till to-morrow night at the same time. I go to
burn the lugger off.'

'I will,' he said; and instantly went off through a gate,
Lizzy continuing her way.

On she tripped at a quickening pace till the lane turned
into the turnpike-road, which she crossed, and got into the
track for Ringsworth. Here she ascended the hill without
the least hesitation, passed the lonely hamlet of Holworth,
and went down the vale on the other side. Stockdale had
never taken any extensive walks in this direction, but he was
aware that if she persisted in her course much longer she
would draw near to the coast, which was here between two
and three miles distant from Nether-Moynton; and as it had
been about a quarter-past eleven o'clock when they set out,
her intention seemed to be to reach the shore about
midnight.

Lizzy soon ascended a small mound, which Stockdale at
the same time adroitly skirted on the left; and a dull monotonous roar burst upon his ear. The hillock was about fifty
yards from the top of the cliffs, and by day it apparently

commanded a full view of the bay. There was light enough in the sky to show her disguised figure against it when she reached the top, where she paused, and afterwards sat down. Stockdale, not wishing on any account to alarm her at this moment, yet desirous of being near her, sank upon his hands and knees, crept a little higher up, and there stayed still.

The wind was chilly, the ground damp, and his position one in which he did not care to remain long. However, before he had decided to leave it, the young man heard voices behind him. What they signified he did not know; but fearing that Lizzy was in danger, he was about to run forward and warn her that she might be seen, when she crept to the shelter of a little bush which maintained a precarious existence in that exposed spot; and her form was absorbed in its dark and stunted outline as if she had become part of it. She had evidently heard the men as well as he. They passed near him, talking in loud and careless tones, which could be heard above the uninterrupted washings of the sea, and which suggested that they were not engaged in any business at their own risk. This proved to be the fact: some of their words floated across to him, and caused him to forget at once the coldness of his situation.

'What's the vessel?'

'A lugger, about fifty tons.'

'From Cherbourg, I suppose?'

'Yes, 'a b'lieve.'

'But it don't all belong to Owlett?'

'O no. He's only got a share. There's another or two in it – a farmer and such like, but the names I don't know.'

The voices died away, and the heads and shoulders of the men diminished towards the cliff, and dropped out of sight.

'My darling has been tempted to buy a share by that unbeliever Owlett,' groaned the minister, his honest affection for Lizzy having quickened to its intensest point during these moments of risk to her person and name. 'That's why she's here,' he said to himself. 'O, it will be the ruin of her!'

His perturbation was interrupted by the sudden bursting out of a bright and increasing light from the spot where Lizzy was in hiding. A few seconds later, and before it had reached the height of a blaze, he heard her rush past him down the hollow like a stone from a sling, in the direction of home. The light now flared high and wide, and showed its position clearly. She had kindled a bough of furze and stuck it into the bush under which she had been crouching; the wind fanned the flame, which crackled fiercely, and threatened to consume the bush as well as the bough. Stockdale paused just long enough to notice thus much, and then followed rapidly the route taken by the young woman. His intention was to overtake her, and reveal himself as a friend; but run as he would he could see nothing of her. Thus he flew across the open country about Holworth, twisting his legs and ankles in unexpected fissures and descents, till, on coming to the gate between the downs and the road, he was forced to pause to get breath. There was no audible movement either in front or behind him, and he now concluded that she had not outrun him, but that, hearing him at her heels, and believing him one of the excise party, she had hidden herself somewhere on the way, and let him pass by.

He went on at a more leisurely pace towards the village. On reaching the house he found his surmise to be correct, for the gate was on the latch, and the door unfastened, just as he had left them. Stockdale closed the door behind him, and waited silently in the passage. In about ten minutes he heard the same light footstep that he had heard in going out; it paused at the gate, which opened and shut softly, and then the door-latch was lifted, and Lizzy came in.

Stockdale went forward and said at once, 'Lizzy, don't be frightened. I have been waiting up for you.'

She started, though she had recognized the voice. 'It is Mr Stockdale, isn't it?' she said.

'Yes,' he answered, becoming angry now that she was

safe indoors, and not alarmed. 'And a nice game I've found you out in to-night. You are in man's clothes, and I am ashamed of you!'

Lizzy could hardly find a voice to answer this unexpected reproach.

'I am only partly in man's clothes,' she faltered, shrinking back to the wall. 'It is only his greatcoat and hat and breeches that I've got on, which is no harm, as he was my own husband; and I do it only because a cloak blows about so, and you can't use your arms. I have got my own dress under just the same – it is only tucked in! Will you go away upstairs and let me pass? I didn't want you to see me at such a time as this!'

'But I have a right to see you! How do you think there can be anything between us now?' Lizzy was silent. 'You are a smuggler,' he continued sadly.

'I have only a share in the run,' she said.

'That makes no difference. Whatever did you engage in such a trade as that for, and keep it such a secret from me all this time?'

'I don't do it always. I only do it in winter-time when 'tis new moon.'

'Well, I suppose that's because it can't be done anywhen else . . . You have regularly upset me, Lizzy.'

'I am sorry for that,' Lizzy meekly replied.

'Well now,' said he more tenderly, 'no harm is done as yet. Won't you for the sake of me give up this blamable and dangerous practice altogether?'

'I must do my best to save this run,' said she, getting rather husky in the throat. 'I don't want to give you up – you know that; but I don't want to lose my venture. I don't know what to do now! Why I have kept it so secret from you is that I was afraid you would be angry if you knew.'

'I should think so! I suppose if I had married you without finding this out you'd have gone on with it just the same?'

'I don't know. I did not think so far ahead. I only went

tonight to burn the folks off, because we found that the preventive-men knew where the tubs were to be landed.'

'It is a pretty mess to be in altogether, is this,' said the distracted young minister. 'Well, what will you do now?'

Lizzy slowly murmured the particulars of their plan, the chief of which were that they meant to try their luck at some other point of the shore the next night; that three landing-places were always agreed upon before the run was attempted, with the understanding that, if the vessel was 'burnt off' from the first point, which was Ringsworth, as it had been by her to-night, the crew should attempt to make the second, which was Lulwind Cove, on the second night; and if there, too, danger threatened, they should on the third night try the third place, which was behind a headland further west.

'Suppose the officers hinder them landing there too?' he said, his attention to this interesting programme displacing for a moment his concern at her share in it.

'Then we shan't try anywhere else all this dark – that's what we call the time between moon and moon – and perhaps they'll string the tubs to a stray-line, and sink 'em a little-ways from shore, and take the bearings; and then when they have a chance they'll go to creep for 'em.'

'What's that?'

'O, they'll go out in a boat and drag a creeper – that's a grapnel – along the bottom till it catch hold of the stray-line.'

The minister stood thinking; and there was no sound within doors but the tick of the clock on the stairs, and the quick breathing of Lizzy, partly from her walk and partly from agitation, as she stood close to the wall, not in such complete darkness but that he could discern against its whitewashed surface the greatcoat, breeches, and broad hat which covered her.

'Lizzy, all this is very wrong,' he said. 'Don't you remember the lesson of the tribute-money? "Render unto Caesar the things that are Caesar's." Surely you have heard that read times enough in your growing up?'

'He's dead,' she pouted.

'But the spirit of the text is in force just the same.'

'My father did it, and so did my grandfather, and almost everybody in Nether-Moynton lives by it, and life would be so dull if it wasn't for that, that I should not care to live at all.'

'I am nothing to live for, of course,' he replied bitterly. 'You would not think it worth while to give up this wild business and live for me alone?'

'I have never looked at it like that.'

'And you won't promise and wait till I am ready?'

'I cannot give you my word to-night.' And looking thoughtfully down, she gradually moved and moved away, going into the adjoining room, and closing the door between them. She remained there in the dark till he was tired of waiting, and had gone up to his own chamber.

Poor Stockdale was dreadfully depressed all the next day by the discoveries of the night before. Lizzy was unmistakably a fascinating young woman, but as a minister's wife she was hardly to be contemplated. 'If I had only stuck to father's little grocery business, instead of going in for the ministry, she would have suited me beautifully!' he said sadly, until he remembered that in that case he would never have come from his distant home to Nether-Moynton, and never have known her.

The estrangement between them was not complete, but it was sufficient to keep them out of each other's company. Once during the day he met her in the garden-path, and said, turning a reproachful eye upon her, 'Do you promise, Lizzy?' But she did not reply. The evening drew on, and he knew well enough that Lizzy would repeat her excursion at night – her half offended manner had shown that she had not the slightest intention of altering her plans at present. He did not wish to repeat his own share of the adventure; but, act as he would, his uneasiness on her account increased with the decline of day. Supposing that an accident should befall her, he would never forgive himself for not being there to help, much as he disliked the idea of seeming to countenance such unlawful escapades.

HOW THEY WENT TO LULWIND COVE

V

As he had expected, she left the house at the same hour at night, this time passing his door without stealth, as if she knew very well that he would be watching, and were resolved to brave his displeasure. He was quite ready, opened the door quickly, and reached the back door almost as soon as she.

'Then you will go, Lizzy?' he said as he stood on the step beside her, who now again appeared as a little man with a face altogether unsuited to his clothes.

'I must,' she said, repressed by his stern manner.

'Then I shall go too,' said he.

'And I am sure you will enjoy it!' she exclaimed in more buoyant tones. 'Everybody does who tries it.'

'God forbid that I should!' he said. 'But I must look after you.'

They opened the wicket and went up the road abreast of each other, but at some distance apart, scarcely a word passing between them. The evening was rather less favourable to smuggling enterprise than the last had been, the wind being lower, and the sky somewhat clear towards the north.

'It is rather lighter,' said Stockdale.

' 'Tis, unfortunately,' said she. 'But it is only from those few stars over there. The moon was new to-day at four o'clock, and I expected clouds. I hope we shall be able to do it this dark, for when we have to sink 'em for long it makes the stuff taste bleachy, and folks don't like it so well.'

Her course was different from that of the preceding night, branching off to the left over Lord's Barrow as soon as they had got out of the lane and crossed the highway. By the time they reached Shaldon Down, Stockdale, who had been in perplexed thought as to what he should say to her, decided that he would not attempt expostulation now, while she was excited by the adventure, but wait till it was over, and endeavour to keep her from such practices in future. It occurred to him once or twice, as they rambled on that should they be surprised by the Preventive-guard, his situation would be more awkward than hers, for it would be difficult to prove his true motive in coming to the spot; but the risk was a slight consideration beside his wish to be with her.

They now arrived at a ravine which lay on the outskirts of Shaldon, a village two miles on their way towards the point of the shore they sought. Lizzy broke the silence this time: 'I have to wait here to meet the carriers. I don't know if they have come yet. As I told you, we go to Lulwind Cove to-night, and it is two miles further than Ringsworth.'

It turned out that the men had already come; for while she spoke two or three dozen heads broke the line of the slope, and a company of them at once descended from the bushes where they had been lying in wait. These carriers were men whom Lizzy and other proprietors regularly employed to bring the tubs from the boat to a hiding-place inland. They were all young fellows of Nether-Moynton, Shaldon, and the neighbourhood, quiet and inoffensive persons, even though some held heavy sticks, who simply engaged to carry the cargo for Lizzy and her cousin Owlett, as they would have engaged in any other labour for which they were fairly well paid.

At a word from her they closed in together. 'You had better take it now,' she said to them; and handed to each a packet. It contained six shillings, their remuneration for the night's undertaking, which was paid beforehand without reference to success or failure; but, besides this, they had the privilege of selling as agents when the run was successfully made. As soon as it was done, she said to them, 'The place is the old one, Dagger's Grave, near Lulwind Cove'; the men till that moment not having been told whither they were bound, for obvious reasons. 'Mr Owlett will meet you there,' added Lizzy. 'I shall follow behind, to see that we are not watched.'

The carriers went on, and Stockdale and Mrs Newberry followed at a distance of a stone's throw. 'What do these men do by day?' he said.

'Twelve or fourteen of them are labouring men. Some are brickmakers, some carpenters, some shoemakers, some thatchers. They are all known to me very well. Nine of 'em are of your own congregation.'

'I can't help that,' said Stockdale.

'Oh, I know you can't. I only told you. The others are more church-inclined, because they supply the pa'son with all the spirits he requires, and they don't wish to show unfriendliness to a customer.'

'How do you choose 'em?' said Stockdale.

'We choose 'em for their closeness, and because they are strong and surefooted, and able to carry a heavy load a long way without being tired.'

Stockdale sighed as she enumerated each particular, for it proved how far involved in the business a woman must be who was so well acquainted with its conditions and needs. And yet he felt more tenderly towards her at this moment than he had felt all the foregoing day. Perhaps it was that her experienced manner and bold indifference stirred his admiration in spite of himself.

'Take my arm, Lizzy,' he murmured.

'I don't want it,' she said. 'Besides, we may never be to each other again what we once have been.'

'That depends upon you,' said he, and they went on again as before.

The hired carriers paced along over Shaldon Down with as little hesitation as if it had been day, avoiding the cart-way, and leaving the village of East Shaldon on the left, so as to reach the crest of the hill at a lonely trackless place not far from the ancient earthwork called Round Pound. A quarter-hour more of brisk walking brought them within sound of the sea, to the place called Dagger's Grave, not many hundred yards from Lulwind Cove. Here they paused, and Lizzy and Stockdale came up with them, when they went on together to the verge of the cliff. One of the men now produced an iron bar, which he drove firmly into the soil a yard from the edge, and attached to it a rope that he had uncoiled from his body. They all began to descend, partly stepping, partly sliding down the incline, as the rope slipped through their hands.

'You will not go to the bottom, Lizzy?' said Stockdale anxiously.

'No. I stay here to watch,' she said. 'Mr Owlett is down there.'

The men remained quite silent when they reached the shore; and the next thing audible to the two at the top was the dip of heavy oars, and the dashing of waves against a boat's bow. In a moment the keel gently touched the shingle, and Stockdale heard the footsteps of the thirty-six carriers running forwards over the pebbles towards the point of landing.

There was a sousing in the water as of a brood of ducks plunging in, showing that the men had not been particular about keeping their legs, or even their waists, dry from the brine: but it was impossible to see what they were doing, and in a few minutes the shingle was trampled again. The iron bar sustaining the rope, on which Stockdale's hand rested, began to swerve a little, and the carriers one by one appeared climbing up the sloping cliff, dripping audibly as they came, and sustaining themselves by the guide-rope. Each man on reaching the top was seen to be carrying a pair of tubs, one on his back and one on his chest, the two being slung together by cords passing round the chine hoops, and resting on the carrier's shoulders. Some of the stronger men carried three by putting an extra one on the top behind, but the customary load was a pair, these being quite weighty enough to give their bearer the sensation of having chest and backbone in contact after a walk of four or five miles.

'Where is Mr Owlett?' said Lizzy to one of them.

'He will not come up this way,' said the carrier. 'He's to bide on shore till we be safe off.' Then, without waiting for the rest, the foremost men plunged across the down; and, when the last had ascended, Lizzy pulled up the rope, wound it round her arm, wriggled the bar from the sod, and turned to follow the carriers.

'You are very anxious about Owlett's safety,' said the minister.

'Was there ever such a man!' said Lizzy. 'Why, isn't he my cousin?'

'Yes. Well, it is a bad night's work,' said Stockdale heavily. 'But I'll carry the bar and rope for you.'

'Thank God, the tubs have got so far all right,' said she.

Stockdale shook his head, and, taking the bar, walked by her side towards the downs; and the moan of the sea was heard no more.

'Is this what you meant the other day when you spoke of having business with Owlett?' the young man asked.

'This is it,' she replied. 'I never see him on any other matter.'

'A partnership of this kind with a young man is very odd.'

'It was begun by my father and his, who were brother-laws.'

Her companion could not blind himself to the fact that where tastes and pursuits were so akin as Lizzy's and Owlett's, and where risks were shared, as with them, in every undertaking, there would be a peculiar appropriateness in her answering Owlett's standing question on matrimony in the affirmative. This did not soothe Stockdale, its tendency being rather to stimulate in him an effort to make the pair as inappropriate as possible, and win her away from this nocturnal crew to correctness of conduct and a minister's parlour in some far-removed inland country.

They had been walking near enough to the file of carriers for Stockdale to perceive that, when they got into the road to the village, they split up into two companies of unequal size, each of which made off in a direction of its own. One company, the smaller of the two, went towards the church, and by the time that Lizzy and Stockdale reached their own house these men had scaled the churchyard wall, and were proceeding noiselessly over the grass within.

'I see that Mr Owlett has arranged for one batch to be put in the church again,' observed Lizzy. 'Do you remember my taking you there the first night you came?'

'Yes, of course,' said Stockdale. 'No wonder you had permission to broach the tubs – they were his, I suppose?'

'No, they were not – they were mine; I had permission from myself. The day after that they went several miles inland in a waggon-load of manure, and sold very well.

At this moment the group of men who had made off to the left some time before began leaping one by one from the hedge opposite Lizzy's house, and the first man, who had no tubs upon his shoulders, came forward.

'Mrs Newberry, isn't it?' he said hastily.

'Yes, Jim,' said she. 'What's the matter?'

'I find that we can't put any in Badger's Clump to-night, Lizzy,' said Owlett. 'The place is watched. We must sling the apple-tree in the orchet if there's time. We can't put any more under the church lumber than I have sent on there, and my mixen hev already more in en than is safe.'

'Very well,' she said. 'Be quick about it – that's all. What can I do?'

'Nothing at all, please. Ah, it is the minister! – you two

that can't do anything had better get indoors and not be zeed.'

While Owlett thus conversed, in a tone so full of contra-band anxiety and so free from lover's jealousy, the men who followed him had been descending one by one from the hedge; and it unfortunately happened that when the hind-most took his leap, the cord slipped which sustained his tubs: the result was that both the kegs fell into the road, one of them being stove in by the blow.

''Od drown it all!' said Owlett, rushing back.

'It is worth a good deal, I suppose?' said Stockdale.

'O no – about two guineas and half to us now,' said Lizzy excitedly. 'It isn't that – it is the smell! It is so blazing strong before it has been lowered by water, that it smells dreadfully when spilt in the road like that! I do hope Latimer won't pass by till it is gone off.'

Owlett and one or two others picked up the burst tub and began to scrape and trample over the spot, to disperse the liquor as much as possible; and then they all entered the gate of Owlett's orchard, which adjoined Lizzy's garden on the right. Stockdale did not care to follow them, for several on recognizing him had looked wonderingly at his presence, though they said nothing. Lizzy left his side and went to the bottom of the garden, looking over the hedge into the orchard, where the men could be dimly seen bustling about, and apparently hiding the tubs. All was done noiselessly, and without a light; and when it was over they dispersed in different directions, those who had taken their cargoes to the church having already gone off to their homes.

Lizzy returned to the garden-gate, over which Stockdale was still abstractedly leaning. 'It is all finished: I am going indoors now,' she said gently. 'I will leave the door ajar for you.'

'O no – you needn't,' said Stockdale; 'I am coming too.'

But before either of them had moved, the faint clatter of horses' hoofs broke upon the ear, and it seemed to come from the point where the track across the down joined the hard road.

'They are just too late!' cried Lizzy exultingly.

'Who?' said Stockdale.

'Latimer, the riding-officer and some assistant of his. We had better go indoors.'

They entered the house, and Lizzy bolted the door. 'Please don't get a light, Mr Stockdale,' she said.

'Of course I will not,' said he.

'I thought you might be on the side of the king,' said Lizzy, with faintest sarcasm.

'I am,' said Stockdale. 'But, Lizzy Newberry, I love you, and you know it perfectly well; and you ought to know, if you do not, what I have suffered in my conscience on your account these last few days!'

'I guess very well,' she said hurriedly. 'Yet I don't see why. Ah, you are better than I!'

The trotting of the horses seemed to have again died away, and the pair of listeners touched each other's fingers in the cold 'Good-night' of those whom something seriously divided. They were on the landing, but before they had taken three steps apart, the tramp of the horsemen suddenly revived, almost close to the house. Lizzy turned to the staircase window, opened the casement about an inch, and put her face close to the aperture. 'Yes, one of 'em is Latimer,' she whispered. 'He always rides a white horse. One would think it was the last colour for a man in that line.'

Stockdale looked, and saw the white shape of the animal as it passed by; but before the riders had gone another ten yards Latimer reined in his horse, and said something to his companion which neither Stockdale nor Lizzy could hear. Its drift was, however, soon made evident, for the other man stopped also; and sharply turning the horses' heads they cautiously retraced their steps. When they were again opposite Mrs Newberry's garden, Latimer dismounted, and the man on the dark horse did the same.

Lizzy and Stockdale, intently listening and observing the proceedings, naturally put their heads as close as possible to the slit formed by the slightly opened casement; and thus it occurred that at last their cheeks came positively into contact. They went on listening, as if they did not know of the singular incident which had happened to their faces, and the pressure of each to each rather increased than lessened with the lapse of time.

They could hear the Customs-men sniffing the air like hounds as they paced slowly along. When they reached the spot where the tub had burst, both stopped on the instant.

'Ay, ay, 'tis quite strong here,' said the second officer. 'Shall we knock at the door?'

'Well, no,' said Latimer. 'Maybe this is only a trick to put us off the scent. They wouldn't kick up this stink anywhere near their hiding-place. I have known such things before.'

'Anyhow, the things, or some of 'em, must have been brought this way,' said the other.

'Yes,' said Latimer musingly. 'Unless 'tis all done to tole us the wrong way. I have a mind that we go home for to-night without saying a word, and come the first thing in the morning with more hands. I know they have storages about here, but we can do nothing by this owl's light. We will look round the parish and see if everybody is in bed, John; and if all is quiet, we will do as I say.'

They went on, and the two inside the window could hear them passing leisurely through the whole village, the street of which curved round at the bottom and entered the turn-pike road at another junction. This way the officers followed, and the amble of their horses died quite away.

'What will you do?' said Stockdale, withdrawing from his position.

She knew that he alluded to the coming search by the officers, to divert her attention from their own tender incident by the casement, which he wished to be passed over as a thing rather dreamt of than done. 'O, nothing,' she replied, with as much coolness as she could command under her disappointment at his manner. 'We often have such storms as this. You would not be frightened if you knew what fools they are. Fancy riding o' horseback through the place; of course they will hear and see nobody while they make that noise; but they are always afraid to get off, in case some of our fellows should burst out upon 'em, and tie them up to the gate-post, as they have done before now. Good-night, Mr Stockdale.'

She closed the window and went to her room, where a tear fell from her eyes; and that not because of the alertness of the riding-officers.

THE GREAT SEARCH AT NETHER-MOYNTON

VI

Stockdale was so excited by the events of the evening, and the dilemma that he was placed in between conscience and love, that he did not sleep, or even doze, but remained as broadly awake as at noonday. As soon as the grey light began to touch ever so faintly the whiter objects in his bedroom he arose, dressed himself, and went downstairs into the road.

The village was already astir. Several of the carriers had heard the well-known canter of Latimer's horse while they were undressing in the dark that night, and had already communicated with each other and Owlett on the subject. The only doubt seemed to be about the safety of those tubs which had been left under the church gallery-stairs, and after a short discussion at the corner of the mill, it was agreed that these should be removed before it got lighter, and hidden in the middle of a double hedge bordering the adjoining field. However, before anything could be carried into effect, the footsteps of many men were heard coming down the lane from the highway.

'Damn it, here they be,' said Owlett, who, having already drawn the hatch and started his mill for the day, stood stolidly at the mill-door covered with flour, as if the interest of his whole soul was bound up in the shaking walls around him.

The two or three with whom he had been talking dispersed to their usual work, and when the Customs-officers, and the formidable body of men they had hired, reached the village cross, between the mill and Mrs Newberry's house, the village wore the natural aspect of a place beginning its morning labours.

'Now,' said Latimer to his associates, who numbered thirteen men in all, 'what I know is that the things are somewhere in this here place. We have got the day before us, and 'tis hard if we can't light upon 'em and get 'em to Budmouth Custom-house before night. First we will try the fuel-houses, and then we'll work our way into the chimmers, and then to the ricks and stables, and so creep round. You have nothing but your noses to guide ye, mind, so use 'em to-day if you never did in your lives before.'

Then the search began. Owlett, during the early part, watched from his mill-window, Lizzy from the door of her house, with the greatest self-possession. A farmer down below, who also had a share in the run, rode about with one eye on his fields and the other on Latimer and his myrmidons, prepared to put them off the scent if he should be asked a question. Stockdale, who was no smuggler at all, felt more anxiety than the worst of them, and went about his studies with a heavy heart, coming frequently to the door to ask Lizzy some question or other on the consequences to her of the tubs being found.

'The consequences,' she said quietly, 'are simply that I shall lose 'em. As I have none in the house or garden, they can't touch me personally.'

'But you have some in the orchard?'

'Mr Owlett rents that of me, and he lends it to others. So

it will be hard to say who put any tubs there if they should be found.'

There was never such a tremendous sniffing known as that which took place in Nether-Moynton parish and its vicinity this day. All was done methodically, and mostly on hands and knees. At different hours of the day they had different plans. From daybreak to breakfast-time the officers used their sense of smell in a direct and straight-forward manner only, pausing nowhere but at such places as the tubs might be supposed to be secreted in at that very moment, pending their removal on the following night. Among the places tested and examined were:

Hollow trees	Cupboards	Culverts
Potato-graves	Clock-cases	Hedgerows
Fuel-houses	Chimney-flues	Faggot-ricks
Bedrooms	Rainwater-butts	Haystacks
Apple-lofts	Pigsties	Coppers and ovens.

After breakfast they recommenced with renewed vigour, taking a new line; that is to say, directing their attention to clothes that might be supposed to have come in contact with the tubs in their removal from the shore, such garments being usually tainted with the spirit, owing to its oozing between the staves. They now sniffed at

Smock-frocks	Smiths' and shoemakers' aprons
Old shirts and waistcoats	Knee-naps and hedging-gloves
Coats and hats	Tarpaulins
Breeches and leggings	Market-cloaks
Women's shawls and gowns	Scarecrows.

And as soon as the mid-day meal was over, they pushed their search into places where the spirits might have been thrown away in alarm:

Horse ponds	Mixens	Sinks in yards
Stable-drains	Wet ditches	Road-scrapings, and
Cinder-heaps	Cesspools	Back-door gutters.

But still these indefatigable Custom-house men discovered nothing more than the original tell-tale smell in the road opposite Lizzy's house, which even yet had not passed off.

'I'll tell ye what it is, men,' said Latimer, about three o'clock in the afternoon, 'we must begin over again. Find them tubs I will.'

The men, who had been hired for the day, looked at their hands and knees, muddy with creeping on all fours so frequently, and rubbed their noses, as if they had almost had enough of it; for the quantity of bad air which had passed into each one's nostril had rendered it nearly as insensible as a flue. However, after a moment's hesitation, they prepared to start anew, except three, whose power of smell had quite succumbed under the excessive wear and tear of the day.

By this time not a male villager was to be seen in the parish. Owlett was not at his mill, the farmers were not in their fields, the parson was not in his garden, the smith had left his forge, and the wheelwright's shop was silent.

'Where the divil are the folk gone?' said Latimer, waking up to the fact of their absence, and looking round. 'I'll have 'em up for this! Why don't they come and help us? There's not a man about the place but the Methodist parson, and he's an old woman. I demand assistance in the king's name!'

'We must find the jineral public afore we can demand that,' said his lieutenant.

'Well, well, we shall do better without 'em,' said Latimer, who changed his moods at a moment's notice. 'But there's great cause of suspicion in this silence and this keeping out of sight, and I'll bear it in mind. Now we will go across to Owlett's orchard and see what we can find there.'

Stockdale, who heard this discussion from the garden-gate, over which he had been leaning, was rather alarmed, and thought it a mistake of the villagers to keep so completely out of the way. He himself, like the Preventives, had been wondering for the last half-hour what could have become of them. Some labourers were of necessity engaged in distant fields, but the master-workmen should have been at home; though one and all, after just showing themselves at their shops, had apparently gone off for the day. He went in to Lizzy, who sat at a back window sewing, and said, 'Lizzy, where are the men?'

Lizzy laughed. 'Where they mostly are when they're run so hard as this.' She cast her eyes to heaven. 'Up there,' she said.

Stockdale looked up. 'What – on top of the church tower?' he asked, seeing the direction of her glance.

'Yes.'

'Well, I expect they will soon have to come down,' said he gravely. 'I have been listening to the officers, and they are going to search the orchard over again, and then every nook in the church.'

Lizzy looked alarmed for the first time. 'Will you go and tell our folk?' she said. 'They ought to be let know.' Seeing his conscience struggling within him like a boiling pot, she added, 'No, never mind, I'll go myself.'

She went out, descended the garden, and climbed over the churchyard wall at the same time that the preventive-men were ascending the road to the orchard. Stockdale could do no less than follow her. By the time that she reached the tower entrance he was at her side, and they entered together.

Nether-Moynton church tower was, as in many villages, without a turret, and the only way to the top was by going up to the singers' gallery, and thence ascending by a ladder to a square trap-door in the floor of the bell-loft, above which a permanent ladder was fixed, passing through the bells to a hole in the roof. When Lizzy and Stockdale reached the gallery and looked up, nothing but the trap-door and the five holes for the bell-ropes appeared. The ladder was gone.

'There's no getting up,' said Stockdale.

'O yes, there is,' said she. 'There's an eye looking at us at this moment through a knot-hole in that trap-door.'

And as she spoke the trap opened, and the dark line of the ladder was seen descending against the white-washed wall. When it touched the bottom Lizzy dragged it to its place, and said, 'If you'll go up, I'll follow.'

The young man ascended and presently found himself among consecrated bells for the first time in his life, nonconformity having been in the Stockdale blood for some generations. He eyed them uneasily, and looked round for Lizzy. Owlett stood here, holding the top of the ladder.

'What, be you really one of us?' said the miller.

'It seems so,' said Stockdale sadly.

'He's not,' said Lizzy, who overheard. 'He's neither for nor against us. He'll do us no harm.'

She stepped up beside them, and then they went on to the next stage, which, when they had clambered over the dusty bell-carriages, was of easy ascent, leading towards the hole through which the pale sky appeared, and into the open air. Owlett remained behind for a moment, to pull up the lower ladder.

'Keep down your heads,' said a voice, as soon as they set foot on the flat.

Stockdale here beheld all the missing parishioners, lying on their stomachs on the tower roof, except a few who, elevated on their hands and knees, were peeping through the embrasures of the parapet. Stockdale did the same, and saw the village lying like a map below him, over which moved the figures of the Customs-men, each foreshortened to a crablike object, the crown of his hat forming a circular disc in the centre of him. Some of the men had turned their heads when the young preacher's figure arose among them.

'What, Mr Stockdale?' said Matt Grey, in a tone of surprise.

'I'd as lief that it hadn't been,' said Jim Clarke. 'If the

pa'son should see him a trespassing here in his tower, 'twould be none the better for we, seeing how 'a do hate chapel-members. He'd never buy a tub of us again, and he's as good a customer as we have got this side o'Warm'll.'

'Where is the pa'son?' said Lizzy.

'In his house, to be sure, that he mid see nothing of what's going on – where all good folks ought to be, and this young man likewise.'

'Well, he has brought some news,' said Lizzy. 'They are going to search the orchard and church; can we do anything if they should find?'

'Yes,' said her cousin Owlett. 'That's what we've been talking o', and we have settled our line. Well, be dazed!'

The exclamation was caused by his perceiving that some of the searchers, having got into the orchard, and begun stooping and creeping hither and thither, were pausing in the middle, where a tree smaller than the rest was growing. They drew closer, and bent lower than ever upon the ground.

'O, my tubs!' said Lizzy faintly, as she peered through the parapet at them.

'They have got 'em, 'a b'lieve,' said Owlett.

The interest in the movements of the officers was so keen that not a single eye was looking in any other direction; but at that moment a shout from the church beneath them attracted the attention of the smugglers, as it did also of the party in the orchard, who sprang to their feet and went towards the church-yard wall. At the same time those of the Government men who had entered the church unperceived by the smugglers cried aloud, 'Here be some of 'em at last.'

The smugglers remained in a blank silence, uncertain whether 'some of 'em' meant tubs or men; but again peeping cautiously over the edge of the tower they learnt that tubs were the things descried; and soon these fated articles were brought one by one into the middle of the churchyard from their hiding-place under the gallery-stairs.

'They are going to put 'em on Hinton's vault till they find the rest!' said Lizzy hopelessly. The Customs-men had, in fact, begun to pile up the tubs on a large stone slab which was fixed there; and when all were brought out from the tower, two or three of the men were left standing by them, the rest of the party again proceeding to the orchard.

The interest of the smugglers in the next manoeuvres of their enemies became painfully intense. Only about thirty tubs had been secreted in the lumber of the tower, but seventy were hidden in the orchard, making up all that they had brought ashore as yet, the remainder of the cargo having been tied to a sinker and dropped overboard for another night's operations. The Preventives, having re-entered the orchard, acted as if they were positive that here lay hidden the rest of the tubs, which they were determined to find before nightfall. They spread themselves out round the fields, and advancing on all fours as before, went anew round every apple-tree in the enclosure. The young tree in the middle again led them to pause, and at length the whole company gathered there in a way which signified that a second chain of reasoning had led to the same results as the first.

When they had examined the sod hereabouts for some minutes, one of the men rose, ran to a disused part of the church where tools were kept, and returned with the sexton's pickaxe and shovel, with which they set to work.

'Are they really buried there?' said the minister, for the grass was so green and uninjured that it was difficult to believe it had been disturbed. The smugglers were too interested to reply, and presently they saw, to their chagrin, the officers stand several on each side of the tree; and, stooping and applying their hands to the soil, they bodily lifted the tree and the turf around it. The apple-tree now showed itself to be growing in a shallow box, with handles for lifting at each of the four sides. Under the site of the tree a square hole was revealed, and an officer went and looked down.

'It is all up now,' said Owlett quietly. 'And now all of ye get down before they notice we are here; and be ready for our next move. I had better bide here till dark, or they may take me on suspicion, as 'tis on my ground. I'll be with ye as soon as daylight begins to pink in.'

'And I?' said Lizzy.

'You please look to the linch-pins and screws; then go indoors and know nothing at all. The chaps will do the rest.'

The ladder was replaced, and all but Owlett descended, the men passing off one by one at the back of the church, and vanishing on their respective errands. Lizzy walked boldly along the street, followed closely by the minister.

'You are going indoors, Mrs Newberry?' he said.

She knew from the words 'Mrs Newberry' that the division between them had widened yet another degree.

'I am not going home,' she said. 'I have a little thing to do before I go in. Martha Sarah will get your tea.'

'O, I don't mean on that account,' said Stockdale. 'What *can* you have to do further in this unhallowed affair?'

'Only a little,' she said.

'What is that? I'll go with you.'

'No, I shall go by myself. Will you please go indoors? I shall be there in less than an hour.'

'You are not going to run any danger, Lizzy?' said the young man, his tenderness reasserting itself.

'None whatever – worth mentioning,' answered she, and went down towards the Cross.

Stockdale entered the garden gate, and stood behind it looking on. The Preventive-men were still busy in the orchard, and at last he was tempted to enter and watch their proceedings. When he came closer he found the secret cellar, of whose existence he had been totally unaware, was formed by timbers placed across from side to side about a foot under the ground, and grassed over.

The officers looked up at Stockdale's fair and downy countenance, and evidently thinking him above suspicion, went on with their work again. As soon as all the tubs were taken out they began tearing up the turf, pulling out the timbers, and breaking in the sides, till the cellar was wholly dismantled and shapeless, the apple-tree lying with its roots high to the air. But the hole which had in its time held so much contraband merchandise was never completely filled up, either then or afterwards, a depression in the greens-ward marking the spot to this day.

THE WALK TO WARM'ELL CROSS AND AFTERWARDS

VII

As the goods had all to be carried to Budmouth that night, the next object of the Custom-house officers was to find horses and carts for the journey, and they went about the village for that purpose. Latimer strode hither and thither with a lump of chalk in his hand, marking broad-arrows so vigorously on every vehicle and set of harness that he came across, that it seemed as if he would chalk broad-arrows on the very hedges and roads. The owner of every conveyance so marked was bound to give it up for Government purposes. Stockdale, who had had enough of the scene, turned indoors thoughtful and depressed. Lizzy was already there, having come in at the back, though she had not yet taken off her bonnet. She looked tired, and her mood was not much brighter than his own. They had but little to say to each other; and the minister went away and attempted to read; but at this he could not succeed, and he shook the little bell for tea.

Lizzy herself brought in the tray, the girl having run off into the village during the afternoon, too full of excitement at the proceedings to remember her state of life. However, almost before the sad lovers had said anything to each other, Martha came in in a steaming state.

'O, there's such a stoor, Mrs Newberry and Mr

Stockdale! The king's officers can't get the carts ready nohow at all! They pulled Thomas Artnell's, and William Rogers's, and Stephen Sprake's carts into the road, and off came the wheels, and down fell the carts; and they found there was no linch-pins in the arms; and then they tried Samuel Shane's waggon, and found that the screws were gone from he, and at last they looked at the dairyman's cart, and he's got none neither! They have gone now to the blacksmith's to get some made, but he's nowhere to be found!'

Stockdale looked at Lizzy, who blushed very slightly, and went out of the room, followed by Martha Sarah. But before they had got through the passage there was a rap at the front door, and Stockdale recognized Latimer's voice addressing Mrs Newberry, who had turned back.

'For God's sake, Mrs Newberry, have you seen Hardman the blacksmith up this way? If we could get hold of him, we'd e'en a'most drag him by the hair of his head to his anvil, where he ought to be.'

'He's an idle man, Mr Latimer,' said Lizzy archly. 'What do you want him for?'

'Why, there isn't a horse in the place that has got more than three shoes on, and some have only two. The waggon-wheels be without strakes, and there's no linch-pins to the carts. What with that, and the bother about every set of harness being out of order, we shan't be off before nightfall – upon my soul we shan't. 'Tis a rough lot, Mrs Newberry, that you've got about you here; but they'll play at this game once too often, mark my words they will! There's not a man in the parish that don't deserve to be whipped.'

It happened that Hardman was at that moment a little further up the lane, smoking his pipe behind a holly-bush. When Latimer had done speaking he went on in this direction, and Hardman, hearing the riding-officer's steps, found curiosity too strong for prudence. He peeped out from the bush at the very moment that Latimer's glance was on it. There was nothing left for him to do but to come forward with unconcern.

'I've been looking for you for the last hour!' said Latimer with a glare in his eye.

'Sorry to hear that,' said Hardman. 'I've been out for a stroll, to look for more hid tubs, to deliver 'em up to Gover'ment.'

'O yes, Hardman, we know it,' said Latimer, with withering sarcasm. 'We know that you'll deliver 'em up to Gover'ment. We know that all the parish is helping us, and have been all day! Now you please walk along with me down to your shop, and kindly let me hire ye in the king's name.'

They went down the lane together; and presently there resounded from the smithy the ring of a hammer not very briskly swung. However, the carts and horses were got into some sort of travelling condition, but it was not until after the clock had struck six, when the muddy roads were glistening under the horizontal light of the fading day. The smuggled tubs were soon packed into the vehicles, and Latimer, with three of his assistants, drove slowly out of the village in the direction of the port of Budmouth, some considerable number of miles distant, the other men of the Preventive-guard being left to watch for the remainder of the cargo, which they knew to have been sunk somewhere between Ringsworth and Lulwind Cove, and to unearth Owlett, the only person clearly implicated by the discovery of the cave.

Women and children stood at the doors as the carts, each chalked with the Government pitchfork, passed in the increasing twilight; and as they stood they looked at the confiscated property with a melancholy expression that told only too plainly the relation which they bore to the trade.

'Well, Lizzy,' said Stockdale, when the crackle of the wheels had nearly died away. 'This is a fit finish to your adventure. I am truly thankful that you have got off without suspicion, and the loss only of the liquor. Will you sit down and let me talk to you?'

'By and by,' she said. 'But I must go out now.'

'Not to that horrid shore again?' he said blankly.

'No, not there. I am only going to see the end of this day's business.'

He did not answer to this, and she moved towards the door slowly, as if waiting for him to say something more.

'You don't offer to come with me,' she added at last. 'I suppose that's because you hate me after all this!'

'Can you say it, Lizzy, when you know I only want to save you from such practices? Come with you! – of course I will, if it is only to take care of you. But why will you go out again?'

'Because I cannot rest indoors. Something is happening, and I must know what. Now, come!' And they went into the dusk together.

When they reached the turnpike-road she turned to the right, and he soon perceived that they were following the direction of the Preventive-men and their load. He had given her his arm, and every now and then she suddenly pulled it back, to signify that he was to halt a moment and listen. They had walked rather quickly along the first quarter of a mile, and on the second or third time of standing still she said, 'I hear them ahead – don't you?'

'Yes,' he said; 'I hear the wheels. But what of that?'

'I only want to know if they get clear away from the neighbourhood.'

'Ah,' said he, a light breaking upon him. 'Something desperate is to be attempted! – and now I remember there was not a man about the village when we left.'

'Hark!' she murmured. The noise of the cartwheels had stopped, and given place to another sort of sound.

' 'Tis a scuffle!' said Stockdale. 'There'll be murder! Lizzy, let go my arm; I am going on. On my conscience, I must not stay here and do nothing!'

'There'll be no murder, and not even a broken head,' she said. 'Our men are thirty to four of them: no harm will be done at all.'

'Then there *is* an attack!' exclaimed Stockdale; 'and you knew it was to be. Why should you side with men who break the laws like this?'

'Why should you side with men who take from country traders what they have honestly bought wi' their own money in France?' said she firmly.

'They are not honestly bought,' said he.

'They are,' she contradicted. 'I and Mr Owlett and the others paid thirty shillings for every one of the tubs before they were put on board at Cherbourg, and if a king who is nothing to us sends his people to steal our property, we have a right to steal it back again.'

Stockdale did not stop to argue the matter, but went quickly in the direction of the noise, Lizzy keeping at his side. 'Don't you interfere, will you, dear Richard?' she said anxiously, as they drew near. 'Don't let us go any closer; 'tis at Warm'ell Cross where they are seizing 'em. You can do no good, and you may meet with a hard blow!'

'Let us see first what is going on,' he said. But before they had got much further the noise of the cartwheels began again, and Stockdale soon found that they were coming towards him. In another minute the three carts came up, and Stockdale and Lizzy stood in the ditch to let them pass.

Instead of being conducted by four men, as had happened when they went out of the village, the horses and carts were now accompanied by a body of from twenty to thirty, all of whom, as Stockdale perceived to his astonishment, had blackened faces. Among them walked six or eight huge female figures, whom, from their wide strides, Stockdale guessed to be men in disguise. As soon as the party discerned Lizzy and her companion four or five fell back, and when the carts had passed, came close to the pair.

'There is no walking up this way for the present,' said one

of the gaunt women, who wore curls a foot long, dangling down the sides of her face, in the fashion of the time. Stockdale recognized this lady's voice as Owlett's.

'Why not?' said Stockdale. 'This is the public highway.'

'Now look here, youngster,' said Owlett. 'O, 'tis the Methodist parson! – what, and Mrs Newberry! Well, you'd better not go up that way, Lizzy. They've all run off, and folks have got their own again.'

The miller then hastened on and joined his comrades. Stockdale and Lizzy also turned back. 'I wish all this hadn't been forced upon us,' she said regretfully. 'But if those Coast-men had got off with the tubs, half the people in the parish would have been in want for the next month or two.'

Stockdale was not paying much attention to her words, and he said, 'I don't think I can go back like this. Those four poor Preventives may be murdered for all I know.'

'Murdered!' said Lizzy impatiently. 'We don't do murder here.'

'Well, I shall go as far as Warm'ell Cross to see,' said Stockdale decisively; and, without wishing her safe home or anything else, the minister turned back. Lizzy stood looking at him till his form was absorbed in the shades; and then, with sadness, she went in the direction of Nether-Moynton.

The road was lonely, and after nightfall at this time of the year there was often not a passer for hours. Stockdale pursued his way without hearing a sound beyond that of his own footsteps; and in due time he passed beneath the trees of the plantation which surrounded the Warm'ell Cross-road. Before he had reached the point of intersection he heard voices from the thicket.

'Hoi-hoi-hoi! Help, help!'

The voices were not at all feeble or despairing, but they were unmistakably anxious. Stockdale had no weapon, and before plunging into the pitchy darkness of the plantation he pulled a stake from the hedge, to use in case of need. When he got among the trees he shouted – 'What's the matter – where are you?'

'Here,' answered the voices; and, pushing through the brambles in that direction, he came near the objects of his search.

'Why don't you come forward?' said Stockdale.

'We be tied to the trees!'

'Who are you?'

'Poor Will Latimer the Customs-officer!' said one plaintively. 'Just come and cut these cords, there's a good man. We were afraid nobody would pass by to-night.'

Stockdale soon loosened them, upon which they stretched their limbs and stood at their ease.

'The rascals!' said Latimer, getting now into a rage, though he had seemed quite meek when Stockdale first came up. ''Tis the same set of fellows. I know they were Moynton chaps to a man.'

'But we can't swear to 'em', said another. 'Not one of 'em spoke.'

'What are you going to do?' said Stockdale.

'I'd fain go back to Moynton, and have at 'em again!' said Latimer.

'So would we!' said his comrades.

'Fight till we die!' said Latimer.

'We will, we will!' said his men.

'But,' said Latimer, more frigidly, as they came out of the plantation, 'we don't *know* that these chaps with black faces were Moynton men? And proof is a hard thing.'

'So it is,' said the rest.

'And therefore we won't do nothing at all,' said Latimer, with complete dispassionateness. 'For my part, I'd sooner be them than we. The clitches of my arms are burning like fire from the cords those two strapping women tied round 'em. My opinion is, now I have had time to think o't, that you may serve your Gover'ment at too high a price. For these two nights and days I have not had an hour's rest;

and, please God, here's for home-along.'

The other officers agreed heartily to this course; and thanking Stockdale for his timely assistance, they parted from him at the Cross, taking themselves the western road, and Stockdale going back to Nether-Moynton.

During that walk the minister was lost in reverie of the most painful kind. As soon as he got into the house, and before entering his own rooms, he advanced to the door of the little back parlour in which Lizzy usually sat with her mother. He found her there alone. Stockdale went forward, and, like a man in a dream, looked down upon the table that stood between him and the young woman, who had her bonnet and cloak still on. As he did not speak, she looked up from her chair at him, with misgiving in her eye.

'Where are they gone?' he then said listlessly.

'Who? – I don't know. I have seen nothing of them since. I came straight in here.'

'If your men can manage to get off with those tubs, it will be a great profit to you, I suppose?'

'A share will be mine, a share my cousin Owlett's, a share to each of the two farmers, and then a share divided amongst the men who helped us.'

'And you still think,' he went on slowly, 'that you will not give this business up?'

Lizzy rose, and put her hand upon his shoulder. 'Don't ask that,' she whispered. 'You don't know what you are asking. I must tell you, though I meant not to do it. What I make by that trade is all I have to keep my mother and myself with.'

He was astonished. 'I did not dream of such a thing,' he said. 'I would rather have scraped the roads, had I been you. What is money compared with a clear conscience?'

'My conscience is clear. I know my mother, but the king I have never seen. His dues are nothing to me. But it is a great deal to me that my mother and I should live.'

'Marry me, and promise to give it up. I will keep your mother.'

'It is good of you,' she said, moved a little. 'Let me think of it by myself. I would rather not answer now.'

She reserved her answer till the next day, and came into his room with a solemn face. 'I cannot do what you wished!' she said passionately. 'It is too much to ask. My whole life ha' been passed in this way.' Her words and manner showed that before entering she had been struggling with herself in private, and that the contention had been strong.

Stockdale turned pale, but he spoke quietly. 'Then, Lizzy, we must part. I cannot go against my principles in this matter, and I cannot make my profession a mockery. You know how I love you, and what I would do for you; but this one thing I cannot do.'

'But why should you belong to that profession?' she burst out. 'I have got this large house; why can't you marry me, and live here with us, and not be a Methodist preacher any more? I assure you, Richard, it is no harm, and I wish you could only see it as I do! We only carry it on in winter: in summer it is never done at all. It stirs up one's dull life at this time o' the year, and gives excitement, which I have got so used to now that I should hardly know how to do 'ithout it. At nights, when the wind blows, instead of being dull and stupid, and not noticing whether it do blow or not, your mind is afield, even if you are not afield yourself; and you are wondering how the chaps are getting on; and you walk up and down the room, and look out o' window, and then you go out yourself, and know your way about as well by night as by day, and have hairbreadth escapes from old Latimer and his fellows, who are too stupid ever to really frighten us, and only make us a bit nimble.'

'He frightened you a little last night, anyhow: and I would advise you to drop it before it is worse.'

She shook her head. 'No, I must go on as I have begun. I was born to it. It is in my blood, and I can't be cured. O, Richard, you cannot think what a hard thing you have asked, and how sharp you try me when you put me between this and my love for 'ee!'

Stockdale was leaning with his elbow on the mantelpiece, his hands over his eyes. 'We ought never to have met, Lizzy,' he said. 'It was an ill day for us! I little thought there was anything so hopeless and impossible in our engagement as this. Well, it is too late now to regret consequences in this way. I have had the happiness of seeing you and knowing you at least.'

'You dissent from Church, and I dissent from State,' she said. 'And I don't see why we are not well matched.'

He smiled sadly, while Lizzy remained looking down, her eyes beginning to overflow.

That was an unhappy evening for both of them, and the days that followed were unhappy days. Both she and he went mechanically about their employments, and his depression was marked in the village by more than one of his denomination with whom he came in contact. But Lizzy, who passed her days indoors, was unsuspected of being the cause: for it was generally understood that a quiet engagement to marry existed between her and her cousin Owlett, and had existed for some time.

Thus uncertainly the week passed on; till one morning Stockdale said to her: 'I have had a letter, Lizzy. I must call you that till I am gone.'

'Gone?' said she blankly.

'Yes,' he said. 'I am going from this place. I felt it would be better for us both that I should not stay after what has happened. In fact, I couldn't stay here, and look on you from day to day, without becoming weak and faltering in my course. I have just heard of an arrangement by which the other minister can arrive here in about a week; and let me go elsewhere.'

That he had all this time continued so firmly fixed in his resolution came upon her as a grievous surprise. 'You never loved me!' she said bitterly.

'I might say the same,' he returned; 'but I will not. Grant me one favour. Come and hear my last sermon on the day before I go.'

Lizzy, who was a church-goer on Sunday mornings, frequently attended Stockdale's chapel in the evening with the rest of the double-minded; and she promised.

It became known that Stockdale was going to leave, and a good many people outside his own sect were sorry to hear it. The intervening days flew rapidly away, and on the evening of the Sunday which preceded the morning of his departure Lizzy sat in the chapel to hear him for the last time. The little building was full to overflowing, and he took up the subject which all had expected, that of the contraband trade so extensively practised among them. His hearers, in laying his words to their own hearts, did not perceive that they were more particularly directed against Lizzy, till the sermon waxed warm, and Stockdale nearly broke down with emotion. In truth his own earnestness, and her sad eyes looking up at him, were too much for the young man's equanimity. He hardly knew how he ended. He saw Lizzy, as through a mist, turn and go away with the rest of the congregation; and shortly afterwards followed her home.

She invited him to supper, and they sat down alone, her mother having, as was usual with her on Sunday nights, gone to bed early.

'We will part friends, won't we?' said Lizzy, with forced gaiety, and never alluding to the sermon: a reticence which rather disappointed him.

'We will,' he said, with a forced smile on his part; and they sat down.

It was the first meal that they had ever shared together in their lives, and probably the last that they would so share. When it was over, and the indifferent conversation could no longer be continued, he arose and took her hand. 'Lizzy,' he said, 'do you say we must part – do you?'

'You do,' she said solemnly. 'I can say no more.'

'Nor I,' said he. 'If that is your answer, good-bye!'

Stockdale bent over her and kissed her, and she involuntarily returned his kiss. 'I shall go early,' he said hurriedly. 'I shall not see you again.'

And he did leave early. He fancied, when stepping forth into the grey morning light, to mount the van which was to carry him away, that he saw a face between the parted curtains of Lizzy's window, but the light was faint, and the panes glistened with wet; so he could not be sure. Stockdale mounted the vehicle, and was gone; and on the following Sunday the new minister preached in the chapel of the Moynton Wesleyans.

One day, two years after the parting, Stockdale, now settled in a midland town, came into Nether-Moynton by carrier in the original way. Jogging along in the van that afternoon he had put questions to the driver, and the answers that he received interested the minister deeply. The result of them was that he went without the least hesitation to the door of his former lodging. It was about six o'clock in the evening, and the same time of year as when he had left; now, too, the ground was damp and glistening, the west was bright, and Lizzy's snowdrops were raising their heads in the border under the wall.

Lizzy must have caught sight of him from the window, for by the time that he reached the door she was there holding it open: and then, as if she had not sufficiently considered her act of coming out, she drew herself back, saying with some constraint, 'Mr Stockdale!'

'You knew it was,' said Stockdale, taking her hand. 'I wrote to say I should call.'

'Yes, but you did not say when,' she answered.

'I did not. I was not quite sure when my business would lead me to these parts.'

'You only came because business brought you near?'

'Well, that is the fact; but I have often thought I should

like to come on purpose to see you . . . But what's all this that has happened? I told you how it would be, Lizzy, and you would not listen to me.'

'I would not,' she said sadly. 'But I had been brought up to that life; and it was second nature to me. However, it is all over now. The officers have blood-money for taking a man dead or alive, and the trade is going to nothing. We were hunted down like rats.'

'Owlett is quite gone, I hear.'

'Yes. He is in America. We had a dreadful struggle that last time, when they tried to take him. It is a perfect miracle that he lived through it; and it is a wonder that I was not killed. I was shot in the hand. It was not by aim; the shot was really meant for my cousin; but I was behind, looking on as usual, and the bullet came to me. It bled terribly, but I got home without fainting; and it healed after a time. You know how he suffered?'

'No,' said Stockdale. 'I only heard that he just escaped with his life.'

'He was shot in the back; but a rib turned the ball. He was badly hurt. We would not let him be took. The men carried him all night across the meads to Kingsbere, and hid him in a barn, dressing his wound as well as they could, till he was so far recovered as to be able to get about. Then he was caught, and tried with the others at the assizes; but they all got off. He had given up his mill for some time; and at last he went to Bristol, and took a passage to America, where he's settled.'

'What do you think of smuggling now?' said the minister gravely.

'I own that we were wrong,' said she. 'But I have suffered for it. I am very poor now, and my mother has been dead these twelve months . . . But won't you come in, Mr Stockdale?'

Stockdale went in; and it is to be supposed that they came to an understanding; for a fortnight later there was a sale of

Lizzy's furniture, and after that a wedding at a chapel in a neighbouring town.

He took her away from her old haunts to the home that he had made for himself in his native county, where she studied her duties as a minister's wife with praiseworthy assiduity. It is said that in after years she wrote an excellent tract called *Render unto Caesar; or, The Repentant Villagers*, in which her own experience was anonymously used as the introductory story. Stockdale got it printed, after making some corrections, and putting in a few powerful sentences of his own; and many hundreds of copies were distributed by the couple in the course of their married life.

AUTHOR'S NOTE. The ending of this story with the marriage of Lizzy and the minister was almost *de rigueur* in an English magazine at the time of writing. But at this late date, thirty years after, it may not be amiss to give the ending that would have been preferred by the writer to the convention used above. Moreover it corresponds more closely with the true incidents of which the tale is a vague and flickering shadow. Lizzy did not, in fact, marry the minister, but – much to her credit in the author's opinion – stuck to Jim the smuggler, and emigrated with him after their marriage, an expatrial step rather forced upon him by his adventurous antecedents. They both died in Wisconsin between 1850 and 1860. (May 1912)

ALSO IN

HEINEMANN
NEW WINDMILLS

General Editors: Anne and Ian Serraillier

Chinua Achebe Things Fall Apart
Douglas Adams The Hitchhiker's Guide to the Galaxy
Vivien Alcock The Cuckoo Sister; The Monster Garden; The Trial of Anna Cotman
Michael Anthony Green Days by the River
Bernard Ashley High Pavement Blues; Running Scared
J G Ballard Empire of the Sun
Stan Barstow Joby
Nina Bawden The Witch's Daughter; A Handful of Thieves; Carrie's War; The Robbers; Devil by the Sea; Kept in the Dark; The Finding; Keeping Henry
Judy Blume It's Not the End of the World; Tiger Eyes
E R Braithwaite To Sir, With Love
John Branfield The Day I Shot My Dad
F Hodgson Burnett The Secret Garden
Ray Bradbury The Golden Apples of the Sun; The Illustrated Man
Betsy Byars The Midnight Fox
Victor Canning The Runaways; Flight of the Grey Goose
John Christopher The Guardians; Empty World
Gary Crew The Inner Circle
Jane Leslie Conly Racso and the Rats of NIMH
Roald Dahl Danny, The Champion of the World; The Wonderful Story of Henry Sugar; George's Marvellous Medicine; The BFG; The Witches; Boy; Going Solo; Charlie and the Chocolate Factory; Matilda
Andrew Davies Conrad's War
Anita Desai The Village by the Sea
Peter Dickinson The Gift; Annerton Pit; Healer
Berlie Doherty Granny was a Buffer Girl
Gerald Durrell My Family and Other Animals
J M Falkner Moonfleet
Anne Fine The Granny Project
F Scott Fitzgerald The Great Gatsby
Anne Frank The Diary of Anne Frank

Leon Garfield Six Apprentices
Graham Greene The Third Man and The Fallen Idol; Brighton Rock
Marilyn Halvorson Cowboys Don't Cry
Thomas Hardy The Withered Arm and Other Wessex Tales
Rosemary Harris Zed
Rex Harley Troublemaker
L P Hartley The Go-Between
Esther Hautzig The Endless Steppe
Ernest Hemingway The Old Man and the Sea; A Farewell to Arms
Nat Hentoff Does this School have Capital Punishment?
Nigel Hinton Getting Free; Buddy; Buddy's Song
Minfong Ho Rice Without Rain
Anne Holm I Am David
Janni Howker Badger on the Barge; Isaac Campion
Kristin Hunter Soul Brothers and Sister Lou
Barbara Ireson (Editor) In a Class of Their Own
Jennifer Johnston Shadows on Our Skin
Toeckey Jones Go Well, Stay Well
James Joyce A Portrait of the Artist as a Young Man
Geraldine Kaye Comfort Herself; A Breath of Fresh Air
Clive King Me and My Million
Dick King-Smith The Sheep-Pig
Daniel Keyes Flowers for Algernon
Elizabeth Laird Red Sky in the Morning
D H Lawrence The Fox and The Virgin and the Gypsy; Selected Tales
Harper Lee To Kill a Mockingbird
Laurie Lee As I Walked Out One Midsummer Morning
Julius Lester Basketball Game
Ursula Le Guin A Wizard of Earthsea
C Day Lewis The Otterbury Incident
David Line Run for Your Life; Screaming High
Joan Lingard Across the Barricades; Into Exile; The Clearance; The File on Fraulein Berg
Penelope Lively The Ghost of Thomas Kempe
Jack London The Call of the Wild; White Fang
Lois Lowry The Road Ahead; The Woods at the End of Autumn Street

How many have you read?